on
fiction

Woolf
on
fiction

'on'

'on'
Published by Hesperus Press Limited
19 Bulstrode Street, London W1U 2JN
www.hesperuspress.com

This collection first published by Hesperus Press Limited, 2011

Designed and typeset by Fraser Muggeridge studio
Printed and bound by CPI Group (UK) Ltd, Croydon CRO 4YY

ISBN: 978-1-84391-618-5

Contents

On Fiction

Hours in a Library

Times Literary Supplement, 30 November 1916.

Let us begin by clearing up the old confusion between the man who loves learning and the man who loves reading, and point out that there is no connexion whatever between the two. A learned man is a sedentary, concentrated solitary enthusiast, who searches through books to discover some particular grain of truth upon which he has set his heart. If the passion for reading conquers him, his gains dwindle and vanish between his fingers. A reader, on the other hand, must check the desire for learning at the outset; if knowledge sticks to him well and good, but to go in pursuit of it, to read on a system, to become a specialist or an authority, is very apt to kill what it suits us to consider the more humane passion for pure and disinterested reading.

In spite of all this we can easily conjure up a picture which does service for the bookish man and raises a smile at his expense. We conceive a pale, attenuated figure in a dressing-gown, lost in speculation, unable to lift a kettle from the hob, or address a lady without blushing, ignorant of the daily news, though versed in the catalogues of the second-hand booksellers, in whose dark premises he spends the hours of sunlight – a delightful character, no doubt, in his crabbed simplicity, but not in the least resembling that other to whom we would direct attention. For the true reader is essentially young. He is a man of intense curiosity; of ideas; open minded and communicative, to whom reading is more of the nature of brisk exercise in the open air than of sheltered study; he trudges the high road, he climbs higher and higher upon the hills until the atmosphere is almost too fine to breathe in; to him it is not a sedentary pursuit at all.

But, apart from general statements, it would not be hard to prove by an assembly of facts that the great season for reading is the season between the ages of eighteen and twenty-four. The bare list of what is read then fills the heart of older people with despair. It is not only that we read so many books, but that we had such books to read. If we wish to refresh our memories, let us take down one of those old notebooks which we have all, at one time or another, had a passion for beginning. Most of the pages are blank, it is true; but at the beginning we shall find a certain number very beautifully covered with a strikingly legible hand-writing. Here we have written down the names of great writers in their order of merit; here we have copied out fine passages from the classics; here are lists of books to be read; and here, most interesting of all, lists of books that have actually been read, as the reader testifies with some youthful vanity by a dash of red ink. We will quote a list of the books that some one read in a past January at the age of twenty, most of them probably for the first time. 1. *Rhoda Fleming*. 2. *The Shaving of Shagpat*. 3. *Tom Jones*. 4. *The Laodicean*. 5. Dewey's *Psychology*. 6. *The Book of Job*. 7. Webbe's *Discourse of Poesie*. 8. *The Duchess of Malfi*. 9. *The Revenger's Tragedy*. And so he goes on from month to month, until, as such lists will, it suddenly stops in the month of June. But if we follow the reader through his months it is clear that he can have done practically nothing but read. Elizabethan literature is gone through with some thoroughness; he read a great deal of Webster, Browning, Shelley, Spenser, and Congreve; Peacock he read from start to finish; and most of Jane Austen's novels two or three times over. He read the whole of Meredith, the whole of Ibsen, and a little of Bernard Shaw. We may be fairly certain, too, that the time not spent in reading was spent in some stupendous argument in which the Greeks were pitted against the moderns, romance against realism, Racine against Shakespeare, until the lights were seen to have grown pale in the dawn.

The old lists are there to make us smile and perhaps to sigh a little, but we would give much to recall also the mood in which this orgy of reading was done. Happily, this reader was no prodigy, and with a little thought we can most of us recall the stages at least of our own initiation. The books we read in childhood, having purloined them from some shelf supposed to be inaccessible, have something of the unreality and awfulness of a stolen sight of the dawn coming over quiet fields when the household is asleep. Peeping between the curtains we see strange shapes of misty trees which we hardly recognize, though we may remember them all our lives; for children have a strange premonition of what is to come. But the later reading of which the above list is an example is quite a different matter. For the first time, perhaps, all restrictions have been removed, we can read what we like; libraries are at our command, and, best of all, friends who find themselves in the same position. For days upon end we do nothing but read. It is a time of extraordinary excitement and exaltation. We seem to rush about recognizing heroes. There is a sort of wonderment in our minds that we ourselves are really doing this, and mixed with it an absurd arrogance and desire to show our familiarity with the greatest human beings who have ever lived in the world. The passion for knowledge is then at its keenest, or at least most confident, and we have, too, an intense singleness of mind which the great writers gratify by making it appear that they are at one with us in their estimate of what is good in life. And as it is necessary to hold one's own against some one who has adopted Pope, let us say, instead of Sir Thomas Browne, for a hero, we conceive a deep affection for these men, and feel that we know them not as other people know them, but privately by ourselves. We are fighting under their leadership, and almost in the light of their eyes. So we haunt the old bookshops and drag home folios and quartos, Euripides in wooden boards, and Voltaire in eighty-nine volumes octavo.

But these lists are curious documents, in that they seem to include scarcely any of the contemporary writers. Meredith and Hardy and Henry James were of course alive when this reader came to them, but they were already accepted among the classics. There is no man of his own generation who influences him as Carlyle, or Tennyson, or Ruskin influenced the young of their day. And this we believe to be very characteristic of youth, for unless there is some admitted giant he will have nothing to do with the smaller men, although they deal with the world he lives in. He will rather go back to the classics, and consort entirely with minds of the very first order. For the time being he holds himself aloof from all the activities of men, and, looking at them from a distance, judges them with superb severity.

Indeed, one of the signs of passing youth is the birth of a sense of fellowship with other human beings as we take our place among them. We should like to think that we keep our standard as high as ever; but we certainly take more interest in the writings of our contemporaries and pardon their lack of inspiration for the sake of something that brings them nearer to us. It is even arguable that we get actually more from the living, although they may be much inferior, than from the dead. In the first place there can be no secret vanity in reading our contemporaries, and the kind of admiration which they inspire is extremely warm and genuine because in order to give way to our belief in them we have often to sacrifice some very respectable prejudice which does us credit. We have also to find our own reasons for what we like and dislike, which acts as a spur to our attention, and is the best way of proving that we have read the classics with understanding.

Thus to stand in a great bookshop crammed with books so new that their pages almost stick together, and the gilt on their backs is still fresh, has an excitement no less delightful than the old excitement of the second-hand bookstall. It is not perhaps so exalted. But the old hunger to know what the immortals thought has given place to a far more tolerant curiosity to know what our own generation is thinking. What do living men and women feel, what are their houses like and what clothes do they wear, what money have they and what food do they eat, what do

6

they love and hate, what do they see of the surrounding world, and what is the dream that fills the spaces of their active lives? They tell us all these things in their books. In them we can see as much both of the mind and of the body of our time as we have eyes for seeing.

When such a spirit of curiosity has fully taken hold of us, the dust will soon lie thick upon the classics unless some necessity forces us to read them. For the living voices are, after all, the ones we understand the best. We can treat them as we treat our equals; they are guessing our riddles, and, what is perhaps more important, we understand their jokes. And we soon develop another taste, unsatisfied by the great – not a valuable taste, perhaps, but certainly a very pleasant possession – the taste for bad books. Without committing the indiscretion of naming names we know which authors can be trusted to produce yearly (for happily they are prolific) a novel, a book of poems or essays, which affords us indescribable pleasure. We owe a great deal to bad books; indeed, we come to count their authors and their heroes among those figures who play so large a part in our silent life. Something of the same sort happens in the case of the memoir writers and autobiographers, who have created almost a fresh branch of literature in our age. They are not all of them important people, but strangely enough, only the most important, the dukes and the statesmen, are ever really dull. The men and women who set out, with no excuse except perhaps that they saw the Duke of Wellington once, to confide to us their opinions, their quarrels, their aspirations, and their diseases, generally end by becoming, for the time at least, actors in those private dramas with which we beguile our solitary walks and our sleepless hours. Refine all this out of our consciousness and we should be poor indeed. And then there are the books of facts and history, books about bees and wasps and industries and gold mines and Empresses and diplomatic intrigues, about rivers and savages, trade unions, and Acts of Parliament, which we always read and always, alas! forget. Perhaps we are not making out a good case for a bookshop when we have to confess that it gratifies so many desires which have apparently nothing to do with literature. But let us remember that here we have a literature in the making. From these new books our children will select the one or two by which we shall be known for ever. Here, if we could recognize it, lies some poem, or novel, or history which will stand up and speak with other ages about our age when we lie prone and silent as the crowd of Shakespeare's day is silent and lives for us only in the pages of his poetry.

This we believe to be true; and yet it is oddly difficult in the case of new books to know which are the real books and what it is that they are telling us, and which are the stuffed books which will come to pieces when they have lain about for a year or two. We can see that there are many books, and we are frequently told that everyone can write nowadays. That may be true; yet we do not doubt that at the heart of this immense volubility, this flood and foam of language, this irreticence and vulgarity and triviality, there lies the heat of some great passion which only needs the accident of a brain more happily turned than the rest to issue in a shape which will last from age to age. It should be our delight to watch this turmoil, to do battle with the ideas and visions of our own time, to seize what we can use, to kill what we consider worthless, and above all to realize that we must be generous to the people who are giving shape as best they can to the ideas within them. No age of literature is so little submissive to authority as ours, so free from the dominion of the great; none seems so wayward with its gift of reverence, or so volatile in its experiments. It may well seem, even to the attentive, that there is no trace of school or aim in the work of our poets and novelists. But the pessimist is inevitable, and he shall not persuade us that our literature is dead, or prevent us from feeling how true and vivid a beauty flashes out as the young writers draw together to form their new vision, the ancient words of the most beautiful of living languages. Whatever we may have learnt from reading the classics we need

8

now in order to judge the work of our contemporaries, for whenever there is life in them they will be casting their net out over some unknown abyss to snare new shapes, and we must throw our imaginations after them if we are to accept with understanding the strange gifts they bring back to us.

But if we need all our knowledge of the old writers in order to follow what the new writers are attempting, it is certainly true that we come from adventuring among new books with a far keener eye for the old. It seems that we should now be able to surprise their secrets; to look deep down into their work and see the parts come together, because we have watched the making of new books, and with eyes clear of prejudice can judge more truly what it is that they are doing, and what is good and what bad. We shall find, probably, that some of the great are less venerable than we thought them. Indeed, they are not so accomplished or so profound as some of our own time. But if in one or two cases this seems to be true, a kind of humiliation mixed with joy overcomes us in front of others. Take Shakespeare, or Milton, or Sir Thomas Browne. Our little knowledge of how things are done does not avail us much here, but it does lend an added zest to our enjoyment. Did we ever in our youngest days feel such amazement at their achievement as that which fills us now that we have sifted myriads of words and gone along uncharted ways in search of new forms for our new sensations? New books may be more stimulating and in some ways more suggestive than the old, but they do not give us that absolute certainty of delight which breathes through us when we come back again to *Comus*, or *Lycidas*, *Urn Burial*, or *Antony and Cleopatra*. Far be it from us to hazard any theory as to the nature of art. It may be that we shall never know more about it than we know by nature, and our longer experience of it teaches us this only – that of all our pleasures those we get from the great artists are indisputably among the best; and more we may not know. But, advancing no theory, we shall find one or two qualities in such works as these which we can hardly expect to find in books made within the span of our lifetime. Age itself may have an alchemy of its own. But this is true: you can read them as often as you will without finding that they have yielded any virtue and left a meaningless husk of words; and there is a complete finality about them. No cloud of suggestions hangs about them teasing us with a multitude of irrelevant ideas. But all our faculties are summoned to the task, as in the great moments of our own experience; and some consecration descends upon us from their hands which we return to life, feeling it more keenly and understanding it more deeply than before.

The Narrow Bridge of Art

New York Herald Tribune, 14 August 1927

Far the greater number of critics turn their backs upon the present and gaze steadily into the past. Wisely, no doubt, they make no comment upon what is being actually written at the moment; they leave that duty to the race of reviewers whose very title seems to imply transiency in themselves and in the objects they survey. But one has sometimes asked oneself, must the duty of the critic always be to the past, must his gaze always be fixed backward? Could he not sometimes turn round and, shading his eyes in the manner of Robinson Crusoe on the desert island, look into the future and trace on its mist the faint lines of the land which some day perhaps we may reach? The truth of such speculations can never be proved, of course, but in an age like ours there is a great temptation to indulge in them. For it is an age clearly when we are not fast anchored where we are; things are moving round us; we are moving ourselves. Is it not the critic's duty to tell us, or to guess at least, where we are going?

Obviously the inquiry must narrow itself very strictly, but it might perhaps be possible in a short space to take one instance of dissatisfaction and difficulty, and, having examined into that, we might be the better able to guess the direction in which, when we have surmounted it, we shall go.

Nobody indeed can read much modern literature without being aware that some dissatisfaction, some difficulty, is lying in our way. On all sides writers are attempting what they cannot achieve, are forcing the form they use to contain a meaning which is strange to it. Many reasons might be given, but here let us select only one, and that is the failure of poetry to serve us as it has served so many generations of our fathers. Poetry is not lending her services to us nearly as freely as she did to them.

The great channel of expression which has carried away so much energy, so much genius, seems to have narrowed itself or to have turned aside.

That is true only within certain limits of course; our age is rich in lyric poetry; no age perhaps has been richer. But for our generation and the generation that is coming the lyric cry of ecstasy or despair, which is so intense, so personal, and so limited, is not enough. The mind is full of monstrous, hybrid, unmanageable emotions. That the age of the earth is 3,000,000,000 years; that human life lasts but a second; that the capacity of the human mind is nevertheless boundless; that life is infinitely beautiful yet repulsive; that one's fellow creatures are adorable but disgusting; that science and religion have between them destroyed belief; that all bonds of union seem broken, yet some control must exist – it is in this atmosphere of doubt and conflict that writers have now to create, and the fine fabric of a lyric is no more fitted to contain this point of view than a rose leaf to envelop the rugged immensity of a rock.

But when we ask ourselves what has in the past served to express such an attitude as this – an attitude which is full of contrast and collision; an attitude which seems to demand the conflict of one character upon another, and at the same time to stand in need of some general shaping power, some conception which lends the whole harmony and force, we must reply that there was a form once, and it was not the form of lyric poetry; it was the form of the drama, of the poetic drama of the Elizabethan age. And that is the one form which seems dead beyond all possibility of resurrection to-day.

For if we look at the state of the poetic play we must have grave doubts that any force on earth can now revive it. It has been practised and is still practised by writers of the highest genius and ambition. Since the death of Dryden every great poet it seems has had his fling. Wordsworth and Coleridge, Shelley and Keats, Tennyson, Swinburne, and Browning (to name the dead only) have all written poetic plays, but none has succeeded. Of all the plays they wrote, probably only Swinburne's *Atalanta* and Shelley's *Prometheus* are still read, and they less frequently than other works by the same writers. All the rest have climbed to the top shelves of our bookcases, put their heads under their wings, and gone to sleep. No one will willingly disturb those slumbers.

Yet it is tempting to try to find some explanation of this failure in case it should throw light upon the future which we are considering. The reason why poets can no longer write poetic plays lies somewhere perhaps in this direction.

There is a vague, mysterious thing called an attitude toward life. We all know people – if we turn from literature to life for a moment – who are at loggerheads with existence; unhappy people who never get what they want; are baffled, complaining, who stand at an uncomfortable angle whence they see everything askew. There are others again who, though they appear perfectly content, seem to have lost all touch with reality. They lavish all their affections upon little dogs and old china. They take interest in nothing but the vicissitudes of their own health and the ups and downs of social snobbery. There are, however, others who strike us, why precisely it would be difficult to say, as being by nature or circumstances in a position where they can use their faculties to the full upon things that are of importance. They are not necessarily happy or successful, but there is a zest in their presence, an interest in their doings. They seem alive all over. This may be partly the result of circumstances – they have been born into surroundings that suit them – but much more is the result of some happy balance of qualities in themselves so that they see things not at an awkward angle, all askew; nor distorted through a mist; but four square, in proportion; they grasp something hard; when they come into action they cut real ice.

A writer too has in the same way an attitude toward life, though it is a different life from the other. They too can stand at an uncomfortable angle; can be baffled, frustrated, unable to get at what they want as writers. This is true, for example, of the novels of George Gissing. Then, again, they can retire to the suburbs and lavish their interest upon pet dogs and duchesses – prettinesses, sentimentalities, snobberies, and this is true of some of our most highly successful novelists. But there are others who seem by nature or circumstances so placed that they can use their faculties freely upon important things. It is not that they write quickly or easily, or become at once successful or celebrated. One is rather trying to analyse a quality which is present in most of the great ages of literature and is most marked in the work of Elizabethan dramatists. They seem to have an attitude toward life, a position which allows them to move their limbs freely; a view which, though made up of all sorts of different things, falls into the right perspective for their purposes.

In part, of course, this was the result of circumstances. The public appetite, not for books, but for the drama, the smallness of the towns, the distance which separated people, the ignorance in which even the educated then lived, all made it natural for the Elizabethan imagination to fill itself with lions and unicorns, dukes and duchesses, violence and mystery. This was reinforced by something which we cannot explain so simply, but which we can certainly feel. They had an attitude toward life which made them able to express themselves freely and fully. Shakespeare's plays are not the work of a baffled and frustrated mind; they are the perfectly elastic envelope of his thought. Without a hitch he turns from philosophy to a drunken brawl; from love songs to an argument; from simple merriment to profound speculation. And it is true of all the Elizabethan dramatists that though they may bore us – and they do – they never make us feel that they are afraid or self-conscious, or that there is anything hindering, hampering, inhibiting the full current of their minds.

Yet our first thought when we open a modern poetic play – and this applies to much modern poetry – is that the writer is not at his ease. He is afraid, he is forced, he is self-conscious. And with what good reason! we may exclaim, for which of us is perfectly at his ease with a man in a toga called Xenocrates, or with a woman in a blanket called Eudoxa? Yet for some reason the modern poetic play is always about Xenocrates and not about Mr Robinson; it is about Thessaly and not about Charing Cross Road. When the Elizabethans laid their scenes in foreign parts and made their heroes and heroines princes and princesses they only shifted the scene from one side to the other of a very thin veil. It was a natural device which gave depth and distance to their figures. But the country remained English; and the Bohemian prince was the same person as the English noble. Our modern poetic playwrights, however, seem to seek the veil of the past and of distance for a different reason. They want not a veil that heightens but a curtain that conceals; they lay their scene in the past because they are afraid of the present. They are aware that if they tried to express the thoughts, the visions, the sympathies and antipathies which are actually turning and tumbling in their brains in this year of grace 1927 the poetic decencies would be violated; they could only stammer and stumble and perhaps have to sit down or to leave the room. The Elizabethans had an attitude which allowed them complete freedom; the modern playwright has either no attitude at all, or one so strained that it cramps his limbs and distorts his vision. He has therefore to take refuge with Xenocrates, who says nothing or only what blank verse can with decency say.

But can we explain ourselves a little more fully? What has changed, what has happened, what has put the writer now at such an angle that he cannot pour his mind straight into the old channels of English poetry? Some sort of answer may be suggested by a walk through the streets of any large town. The long avenue of brick is cut up into boxes, each of which is inhabited by a different human being who has put locks on his doors and bolts on his windows to ensure some privacy, yet is linked to his fellows by wires which pass overhead, by waves of sound which pour through the roof and speak aloud to him of battles and murders and strikes and revolutions all over the world. And if we go in and talk to him we shall find that he is a wary, secretive, suspicious animal, extremely self-conscious, extremely careful not to give himself away. Indeed, there is nothing in modern life which forces him to do it. There is no violence in private life; we are polite, tolerant, agreeable, when we meet. War even is conducted by companies and communities rather than by individuals. Duelling is extinct. The marriage bond can stretch indefinitely without snapping. The ordinary person is calmer, smoother, more self-contained than he used to be.

But again we should find if we took a walk with our friend that he is extremely alive to everything – to ugliness, sordidity, beauty, amusement. He follows every thought careless where it may lead him. He discusses openly what used never to be mentioned even privately. And this very freedom and curiosity are perhaps the cause of what appears to be his most marked characteristic – the strange way in which things that have no apparent connection are associated in his mind. Feelings which used to come single and separate do so no longer. Beauty is part ugliness; amusement part disgust; pleasure part pain. Emotions which used to enter the mind whole are now broken up on the threshold.

For example: it is a spring night, the moon is up, the night-ingale singing, the willows bending over the river. Yes, but at the same time a diseased old woman is picking over her greasy rags on a hideous iron bench. She and the spring enter his mind together; they blend but do not mix. The two emotions, so incongruously coupled, bite and kick at each other in unison. But the emotion which Keats felt when he heard the song of the nightingale is one and entire, though it passes from joy in beauty to sorrow at the unhappiness of human fate. He makes no contrast. In his poem sorrow is the shadow which accompanies beauty. In the modern mind beauty is accompanied not by its shadow but by its opposite. The modern poet talks of the nightingale who sings 'jug jug to dirty ears'. There trips along by the side of our modern beauty some mocking spirit which sneers at beauty for being beautiful; which turns the looking-glass and shows us that the other side of her cheek is pitted and deformed. It is as if the modern mind, wishing always to verify its emotions, had lost the power of accepting anything simply for what it is. Undoubtedly this sceptical and testing spirit has led to a great freshening and quickening of soul. There is a candour, an honesty in modern writing which is salutary if not supremely delightful. Modern literature, which had grown a little sultry and scented with Oscar Wilde and Walter Pater, revived instantly from her nineteenth-century languor when Samuel Butler and Bernard Shaw began to burn their feathers and apply their salts to her nose. She awoke; she sat up; she sneezed. Naturally, the poets were frightened away.

For of course poetry has always been overwhelmingly on the side of beauty. She has always insisted on certain rights, such as rhyme, metre, poetic diction. She has never been used for the common purpose of life. Prose has taken all the dirty work on to her own shoulders; has answered letters, paid bills, written articles, made speeches, served the needs of businessmen, shop-keepers, lawyers, soldiers, peasants.

Poetry has remained aloof in the possession of her priests. She has perhaps paid the penalty for this seclusion by becoming a little stiff. Her presence with all her apparatus – her veils, her garlands, her memories, her associations – affects us the moment she speaks. Thus when we ask poetry to express this discord, this incongruity, this sneer, this contrast, this curiosity, the quick, queer emotions which are bred in small separate rooms, the wide, general ideas which civilization teaches, she cannot move quickly enough, simply enough, or broadly enough to do it. Her accent is too marked; her manner too emphatic. She gives us instead lovely lyric cries of passion; with a majestic sweep of her arm she bids us take refuge in the past;

[handwritten marginal note: Personal statement]

but she does not keep pace with the mind and fling herself subtly, quickly, passionately into its various sufferings and joys. Byron in *Don Juan* pointed the way; he showed how flexible an instrument poetry might become, but none has followed his example or put his tool to further use. We remain without a poetic play.

Thus we are brought to reflect whether poetry is capable of the task which we are now setting her. It may be that the emotions here sketched in such rude outline and imputed to the modern mind submit more readily to prose than to poetry. It may be possible that prose is going to take over – has, indeed, already taken over – some of the duties which were once discharged by poetry.

If, then, we are daring and risk ridicule and try to see in what direction we who seem to be moving so fast are going, we may guess that we are going in the direction of prose and that in ten or fifteen years' time prose will be used for purposes for which prose has never been used before. That cannibal, the novel, which has devoured so many forms of art will by then have devoured even more. We shall be forced to invent new names for the different books which masquerade under this one heading. And it is possible that there will be among the so-called novels one which we shall scarcely know how to christen. It will be written in prose, but in prose which has many of the characteristics of poetry. It will have something of the exaltation of poetry, but much of the ordinariness of prose. It will be dramatic, and yet not a play. It will be read, not acted. By what name we are to call it is not a matter of very great importance. What is important is that this book which we see on the horizon may serve to express some of those feelings which seem at the moment to be balked by poetry pure and simple and to find the drama equally inhospitable to them. Let us try, then, to come to closer terms with it and to imagine what may be its scope and nature.

In the first place, one may guess that it will differ from the novel as we know it now chiefly in that it will stand further back from life. It will give, as poetry does, the outline rather than the detail. It will make little use of the marvellous fact-recording power, which is one of the attributes of fiction. It will tell us very little about the houses, incomes, occupations of its characters; it will have little kinship with the sociological novel or the novel of environment. With these limitations it will express the feeling and ideas of the characters closely and vividly, but from a different angle. It will resemble poetry in this that it will give not only or mainly people's relations to each other and their activities together, as the novel has hitherto done, but it will give the relation of the mind to general ideas and its soliloquy in solitude. For under the dominion of the novel we have scrutinized one part of the mind closely and left another unexplored. We have come to forget that a large and important part of life consists in our emotions toward such things as roses and nightingales, the dawn, the sunset, life, death, and fate; we forget that we spend much time sleeping, dreaming, thinking, reading, alone; we are not entirely occupied in personal relations; all our energies are not absorbed in making our livings. The psychological novelist has been too prone to limit psychology to the psychology of personal intercourse; we long sometimes to escape from the incessant, the remorseless analysis of falling into love and falling out of love, of what Tom feels for Judith and Judith does or does not altogether feel for Tom. We long for some more impersonal relationship. We long for ideas, for dreams, for imaginations, for poetry.

And it is one of the glories of the Elizabethan dramatists that they give us this. The poet is always able to transcend the particularity of Hamlet's relation to Ophelia and to give us his questioning not of his own personal lot alone but of the state and being of all human life. In *Measure for Measure*, for example, passages of extreme psychological subtlety are mingled with profound reflections, tremendous imaginations. Yet it is worth noticing that if Shakespeare gives us this profundity, this psychology, at the same time Shakespeare makes no attempt to give us certain other things. The plays are of no use whatever as 'applied sociology'. If we had to depend upon them for a knowledge of the social and economic conditions of Elizabethan life, we should be hopelessly at sea.

In these respects then the novel or the variety of the novel which will be written in time to come will take on some of the attributes of poetry. It will give the relations of man to nature, to fate; his imagination; his dreams. But it will also give the sneer, the contrast, the question, the closeness and complexity of life. It will take the mould of that queer conglomeration of incongruous things – the modern mind. Therefore it will clasp to its breast the precious prerogatives of the democratic art of prose; its freedom, its fearlessness, its flexibility. For prose is so humble that it can go anywhere; no place is too low, too sordid, or too mean for it to enter. It is infinitely patient, too, humbly acquisitive. It can lick up with its long glutinous tongue the most minute fragments of fact and mass them into the most subtle labyrinths, and listen silently at doors behind which only a murmur, only a whisper, is to be heard. With all the suppleness of a tool which is in constant use it can follow the windings and record the changes which are typical of the modern mind. To this, with Proust and Dostoevsky behind us, we must agree.

But can prose, we may ask, adequate though it is to deal with the common and the complex – can prose say the simple things which are so tremendous? Give the sudden emotions which are so surprising? Can it chant the elegy, or hymn the love, or shriek in terror, or praise the rose, the nightingale, or the beauty of the night? Can it leap at one spring at the heart of its subject as the poet does? I think not. That is the penalty it pays for having dispensed with the incantation and the mystery, with rhyme and metre. It is true that prose writers are daring; they are constantly forcing their instrument to make the attempt. But one has always a feeling of discomfort in the presence of the purple patch or the prose poem. The objection to the purple patch, however, is not that it is purple but that it is a patch. Recall

[Handwritten marginalia: "why poetry important too"]

for instance Meredith's 'Diversion on a Penny Whistle' in *Richard Feverel*. How awkwardly, how emphatically, with a broken poetic metre it begins: 'Golden lie the meadows; golden run the streams; red-gold is on the pine-stems. The sun is coming down to earth and walks the fields and the waters.' Or recall the famous description of the storm at the end of Charlotte Brontë's *Villette*. These passages are eloquent, lyrical, splendid; they read very well cut out and stuck in an anthology; but in the context of the novel they make us uncomfortable. For both Meredith and Charlotte Brontë called themselves novelists; they stood close up to life; they led us to expect the rhythm, the observation, and the perspective of prose. We feel the jerk and the effort; we are half woken from that trance of consent and illusion in which our submission to the power of the writer's imagination is most complete.

But let us now consider another book, which though written in prose and by way of being called a novel, adopts from the start a different attitude, a different rhythm, which stands back from life, and leads us to expect a different perspective – *Tristram Shandy*. It is a book full of poetry, but we never notice it; it is a book stained deep purple, which is yet never patchy. Here though the mood is changing always, there is no jerk, no jolt in that change to waken us from the depths of consent and belief. In the same breath Sterne laughs, sneers, cuts some indecent ribaldry, and passes on to a passage like this:

Time wastes too fast: every letter I trace tells me with what rapidity life follows my pen; the days and hours of it more precious – my dear Jenny – than the rubies about thy neck, are flying over our heads like light clouds of a windy day, never to return more; everything presses on – whilst thou are twisting that lock – see! it grows gray; and every time I kiss thy hand to bid adieu, and every absence which follows it, are preludes to that eternal separation which we are shortly to make. – Heaven have mercy upon us both!

CHAP. IX

Now, for what the world thinks of that ejaculation – I would not give a groat.

And he goes on to my Uncle Toby, the Corporal, Mrs Shandy, and the rest of them.

There, one sees, is poetry changing easily and naturally into prose, prose into poetry. Standing a little aloof, Sterne lays his hands lightly upon imagination, wit, fantasy; and reaching high up among the branches where these things grow, naturally and no doubt willingly forfeits his right to the more substantial vegetables that grow on the ground. For, unfortunately, it seems true that some renunciation is inevitable. You cannot cross the narrow bridge of art carrying all its tools in your hands. Some you must leave behind, or you will drop them in midstream or, what is worse, overbalance and be drowned yourself.

So, then, this unnamed variety of the novel will be written standing back from life, because in that way a larger view is to be obtained of some important features of it; it will be written in prose, because prose, if you free it from the beast-of-burden work which so many novelists necessarily lay upon it, of carrying loads of details, bushels of fact – prose thus treated will show itself capable of rising high from the ground, not in one dart, but in sweeps and circles, and of keeping at the same time in touch with the amusements and idiosyncrasies of human character in daily life.

There remains, however, a further question. Can prose be dramatic? It is obvious, of course, that Shaw and Ibsen have used prose dramatically with the highest success, but they have been faithful to the dramatic form. This form one may prophesy is not the one which the poetic dramatist of the future will find fit for his needs. A prose play is too rigid, too limited, too emphatic for his purposes. It lets slip between its meshes half the things that he wants to say. He cannot compress into dialogue all the comment, all the analysis, all the richness that he wants to give.

Yet he covets the explosive emotional effect of the drama; he wants to draw blood from his readers, and not merely to stroke and tickle their intellectual susceptibilities. The looseness and freedom of *Tristram Shandy*, wonderfully though they encircle and float off such characters as Uncle Toby and Corporal Trim, do not attempt to range and marshal these people in dramatic contrast together. Therefore it will be necessary for the writer of this exacting book to bring to bear upon his tumultuous and contradictory emotions the generalizing and simplifying power of a strict and logical imagination. Tumult is vile; confusion is hateful; everything in a work of art should be mastered and ordered. His effort will be to generalize and split up. Instead of enumerating details he will mould blocks. His characters thus will have a dramatic power which the minutely realized characters of contemporary fiction often sacrifice in the interests of psychology. And then, though this is scarcely visible, so far distant it lies on the rim of the horizon – one can imagine that he will have extended the scope of his interest so as to dramatize some of those influences which play so large a part in life, yet have so far escaped the novelist – the power of music, the stimulus of sight, the effect on us of the shape of trees or the play of colour, the emotions bred in us by crowds, the obscure terrors and hatreds which come so irrationally in certain places or from certain people, the delight of movement, the intoxication of wine. Every moment is the centre and meeting-place of an extraordinary number of perceptions which have not yet been expressed. Life is always and inevitably much richer than we who try to express it.

But it needs no great gift of prophecy to be certain that whoever attempts to do what is outlined above will have need of all his courage. Prose is not going to learn a new step at the bidding of the first comer. Yet if the signs of the times are worth anything the need of fresh developments is being felt. It is certain that there are scattered about in England, France, and America writers who are trying to work themselves free from a bondage which has become irksome to them; writers who are trying to readjust their attitude so that they may once more stand easily and naturally in a position where their powers have full play upon important things. And it is when a book strikes us as the result of that attitude rather than by its beauty or its brilliancy that we know that it has in it the seeds of an enduring existence.

Phases of Fiction

The Bookman, April, May & June 1929

The following pages attempt to record the impressions made upon the mind by reading a certain number of novels in succession. In deciding which book to begin with and which book to go on with, the mind was not pressed to make a choice. It was allowed to read what it liked. It was not, that is to say, asked to read historically, nor was it asked to read critically. It was asked to read only for interest and pleasure, and, at the same time, to comment as it read upon the nature of the interest and the pleasure that it found. It went its way, therefore, independent of time and reputation. It read Trollope before it read Jane Austen and skipped, by chance or negligence, some of the most celebrated books in English fiction. Thus, there is little reference or none to Fielding, Richardson, or Thackeray.

Yet, if nobody save the professed historian and critic reads to understand a period or to revise a reputation, nobody reads simply by chance or without a definite scale of values. There is, to speak metaphorically, some design that has been traced upon our minds which reading brings to light. Desires, appetites, however we may come by them, fill it in, scoring now in this direction, now in that. Hence, an ordinary reader can often trace his course through literature with great exactness and can even think himself, from time to time, in possession of a whole world as inhabitable as the real world. Such a world, it may be urged against it, is always in process of creation. Such a world, it may be added, likewise against it, is a personal world, a world limited and unhabitable perhaps by other people, a world created in obedience to tastes that may be peculiar to one temperament and distasteful to another – indeed, any such record of reading, it will be concluded, is bound to be limited, personal, erratic.

In its defence, however, it may be claimed that if the critic and the historian speak a more universal language, a more learned language, they are also likely to miss the centre and to lose their way for the simple reason that they know so many things about a writer that a writer does not know about himself. Writers are heard to complain that influences – education, heredity, theory – are given weight of which they themselves are unconscious in the act of creation. Is the author in question the son of an architect or a bricklayer? Was he educated at home or at the university? Does he come before or after Thomas Hardy? Yet not one of these things is in his mind, perhaps, as he writes and the reader's ignorance, narrowing and limiting as it is, has at least the advantage that it leaves unhampered what the reader has in common with the writer, though much more feebly: the desire to create.

Here, then, very briefly and with inevitable simplifications, an attempt is made to show the mind at work upon a shelf full of novels and to watch it as it chooses and rejects, making itself a dwelling-place in accordance with its own appetites. Of these appetites, perhaps, the simplest is the desire to believe wholly and entirely in something which is fictitious. That appetite leads on all the others in turn. There is no saying, for they change so much at different ages, that one appetite is better than another. The common reader is, moreover, suspicious of fixed labels and settled hierarchies. Still, since there must be an original impulse, let us give the lead to this one and start upon the shelf full of novels in order to gratify our wish to believe.

The Truth-Tellers

In English fiction there are a number of writers who gratify our sense of belief – Defoe, Swift, Trollope, Borrow, W.E. Norris, for example; among the French, one thinks instantly of Maupassant. Each of them assures us that things are precisely as they say they are. What they describe happens actually before our eyes. We get from their novels the same sort of refreshment and delight that we get from seeing something actually happen in the street below. A dustman, for example, by an awkward movement of his arm knocks over a bottle apparently containing Condy's Fluid which cracks upon the pavement. The dustman gets down; he picks up the jagged fragments of the broken bottle; he turns to a man who is passing in the street. We cannot take our eyes off him until we have feasted our powers of belief to the full. It is as if a channel were cut, into which suddenly and with great relief an emotion hitherto restrained rushes and pours. We forget whatever else we may be doing. This positive experience overpowers all the mixed and ambiguous feelings of which we may be possessed at the moment. The dustman has knocked over a bottle; the red stain is spreading on the pavement. It happens precisely so.

The novels of the great truth-tellers, of whom Defoe is easily the English chief, procure for us a refreshment of this kind. He tells us the story of Moll Flanders, of Robinson Crusoe, of Roxana, and we feel our powers of belief rush into the channel, thus cut, instantly, fertilizing and refreshing our entire being. To believe seems the greatest of all pleasures. It is impossible to glut our greed for truth, so rapacious is it. There is not a shadowy or insubstantial word in the whole book to startle our nervous sense of security. Three or four strong, direct strokes of the pen carve out Roxana's character. Her dinner is set indisputably on the table. It consists of veal and turnips. The day is fine or cloudy; the month is April or September. Persistently, naturally, with a curious, almost unconscious iteration, emphasis is laid upon the very facts that most reassure us of stability in real life, upon money, furniture, food, until we seem wedged among solid objects in a solid universe.

One element of our delight comes from the sense that this world, with all its circumstantiality, bright and round and hard as it is, is yet complete, so that in whatever direction we reach out for assurance we receive it. If we press on beyond the confines of each page, as it is our instinct to do, completing what the writer has left unsaid, we shall find that we can trace our way; that there are indications which let us realize them; there is an under side, a dark side to this world. Defoe presided over his universe with the omnipotence of a God, so that his world is perfectly in scale. Nothing is so large that it makes another thing too small; nothing so small that it makes another thing too large.

The name of God is often found on the lips of his people, but they invoke a deity only a little less substantial than they are themselves, a being seated solidly not so very far above them in the tree tops. A divinity more mystical, could Defoe have made us believe in him, would so have discredited the landscape and cast doubt upon the substance of the men and women that our belief in them would have perished at the heart. Or, suppose that he let himself dwell upon the green shades of the forest depths or upon the sliding glass of the summer stream. Again, however much we were delighted by the description, we should have been uneasy because this other reality would have wronged the massive and monumental reality of Crusoe and Moll Flanders. As it is, saturated with the truth of his own universe, no such discrepancy is allowed to intrude. God, man, nature are all real, and they are all real with the same kind of reality – an astonishing feat, since it implies complete and perpetual submission on the writer's part to his conviction, an obdurate deafness to all the voices which seduce and tempt him to gratify other moods. We have only to reflect how seldom a book is carried through on the same impulse of belief, so that its perspective is harmonious throughout, to realize how great a writer Defoe was. One could number on one's fingers half a dozen novels which set out to be masterpieces and yet have failed because the belief flags; the realities are mixed; the perspective shifts and, instead of a final clarity, we get a baffling, if only a momentary, confusion.

Having, now, feasted our powers of belief to the full and so enjoyed the relief and rest of this positive world existing so palpably and completely outside of us, there begins to come over us that slackening of attention which means that the nerve in use is sated for the time being. We have absorbed as much of this literal truth as we can and we begin to crave for something to vary it that will yet be in harmony with it We do not want, except in a flash or a hint, such truth as Roxana offers us when she tells us how her master, the Prince, would sit by their child and 'loved to look at it when it was asleep'. For that truth is hidden truth; it makes us dive beneath the surface to realize it and so holds up the action. It is, then, action that we want. One desire having run its course, another leaps forward to take up the burden and no sooner have we formulated our desire than Defoe has given it to us. 'On with the story' – that cry is forever on his lips. No sooner has he got his facts assembled than the burden is floated. Perpetually springing up, fresh and effortless, action and event, quickly succeeding each other thus set in motion this dense accumulation of facts and keep the breeze blowing in our faces. It becomes obvious, then, that if his people are sparely equipped and bereft of certain affections, such as love of husband and child, which we expect of people at leisure, it is that they may move quicker. They must travel light since it is for adventure that they are made. They will need quick wits, strong muscles, and rocky common sense on the road they are to travel rather than sentiment, reflection, or the power of self-analysis.

Belief, then, is completely gratified by Defoe. Here, the reader can rest himself and enter into possession of a large part of his domain. He tests it; he tries it; he feels nothing give under him or fade before him. Still, belief seeks fresh sustenance as a sleeper seeks a fresh side of the pillow. He may turn, and this is likely, to someone closer to him in time than Defoe in order to gratify his desire for belief (for distance of time in a novel sets up picturesqueness, hence unfamiliarity).

If he should take down, for example, some book of a prolific and once esteemed novelist, like W.E. Norris, he will find that the juxtaposition of the two books brings each out more clearly.

W.E. Norris was an industrious writer who is well worth singling out for inquiry if only because he represents that vast body of forgotten novelists by whose labours fiction is kept alive in the absence of the great masters. At first, we seem to be given all that we need: girls and boys, cricket, shooting, dancing, boating, lovemaking, marriage; a park here; a London drawing-room there; here, an English gentleman; there, a cad; dinners, tea-parties, canters in the Row; and, behind it all, green and gray, domestic and venerable, the fields and manor houses of England. Then, as one scene succeeds another, halfway through the book, we seem to have a great deal more belief on our hands than we know what to do with. We have exhausted the vividness of slang; the modernity, the adroit turn of mood. We loiter on the threshold of the scene, asking to be allowed to press a little further; we take some phrase, and look at it as if it ought to yield us more. Then, turning our eyes from the main figures, we try to sketch out something in the background, to pursue these feelings and relations away from the present moment; not, needless to say, with a view to discovering some over-arching conception, something which we may call 'a reading of life'. No, our desire is otherwise: some shadow of depth appropriate to the bulk of the figures; some Providence such as Defoe provides or morality such as he suggests, so that we can go beyond the age itself without falling into inanity.

Then, we discover it is the mark of a second-rate writer that he cannot pause here or suggest there. All his powers are strained in keeping the scene before us, its brightness and its credibility. The surface is all; there is nothing beyond.

Our capacity for belief, however, is not in the least exhausted. It is only a question of finding something that will revive it for us. Not Shakespeare and not Shelley and not Hardy; perhaps, Trollope, Swift, Maupassant. Above all, Maupassant is the most promising at the moment, for Maupassant enjoys the great advantage that he writes in French. Not from any merit of his own, he gives us that little fillip which we get from reading a language whose edges have not been smoothed for us by daily use. The very sentences shape themselves in a way that is definitely charming. The words tingle and sparkle. As for English, alas, it is *our* language – shop-worn, not so desirable, perhaps. Moreover, each of these compact little stories has its pinch of gunpowder, artfully placed so as to explode when we tread on its tail. The last words are always highly charged. Off they go, *bang*, in our faces and there is lit up for us in one uncompromising glare someone with his hand lifted, someone sneering, someone turning his back, someone catching an omnibus, as if this insignificant action, whatever it may be, summed up the whole situation forever.

The reality that Maupassant brings before us is always one of the body, of the senses – the ripe flesh of a servant girl, for example, or the succulence of food. 'Elle restait inerte, ne sentant plus son corps, et l'esprit dispersé, comme si quelqu'un l'eût déchiqueté avec un de ces instruments dont se servent les cardeurs pour effiloquer la laine des matelas.'[1] Or her tears dried themselves upon her cheeks 'comme des gouttes d'eau sur du fer rouge'.[2] It is all concrete; it is all visualized. It is a world, then, in which one can believe with one's eyes and one's nose and one's senses; nevertheless, it is a world which secretes per-petually a little drop of bitterness. Is this all? And, if this is all, is it enough? Must we, then, believe this? So we ask. Now that we are given truth unadorned, a disagreeable sensation seems attached to it, which we must analyse before we go further.

Suppose that one of the conditions of things as they are is that they are unpleasant, have we strength enough to support that unpleasantness for the sake of the delight of believing in it? Are we not shocked somehow by *Gulliver's Travels* and *Boule de suif* and *La Maison Tellier*? Shall we not always be trying to get round the obstacle of ugliness by saying that Maupassant and his like are narrow, cynical, and unimaginative when, in fact, it is their truthfulness that we resent – the fact that leeches suck the naked legs of servant girls, that there are brothels, that human nature is fundamentally cold, selfish, corrupt? This discomfort at the disagreeableness of truth is one of the first things that shakes very lightly our desire to believe. Our Anglo-Saxon blood, perhaps, has given us an instinct that truth is, if not exactly beautiful, at least pleasant or virtuous to behold. But let us look once more at truth and, this time, through the eyes of Anthony Trollope, 'a big, blustering, spectacled, loud voiced hunting man... whose language in male society was, I believe, so lurid that I was not admitted to breakfast with him...who rode about the country establishing penny posts, and wrote, as the story goes, so many thousand words before breakfast every day of his life'.*

Certainly, the Barchester novels tell the truth, and the English truth, at first sight, is almost as plain of feature as the French truth, though with a difference. Mr Slope is a hypocrite, with a 'pawing, greasy way with him'. Mrs Proudie is a domineering bully. The Archdeacon is well-meaning but coarse-grained and thick-cut. Thanks to the vigour of the author, the world of which these are the most prominent inhabitants goes through its daily rigmarole of feeding and begetting children and worshipping with a thoroughness, a gusto, which leave us no loophole of escape. We believe in Barchester as we believe in the reality of our own weekly bills. Nor, indeed, do we wish to escape from the consequences of our belief, for the truth of the Slopes and the Proudies, the truth of the evening party where Mrs Proudie has her dress torn off her back under the light of eleven gas jets, is entirely acceptable.

At the top of his bent Trollope is a big, if not first-rate novelist, and the top of his bent came when he drove his pen hard and fast after the humours of provincial life and scored, without cruelty but with hale and hearty common sense, the

* *Vignettes of Memory* by Lady Violet Greville, 1927.

portraits of those well-fed, black-coated, unimaginative men and women of the fifties. In his manner with them, and his manner is marked, there is an admirable shrewdness, like that of a family doctor or solicitor, too well acquainted with human foibles to judge them other than tolerantly and not above the human weakness of liking one person a great deal better than another for no good reason. Indeed, though he does his best to be severe and is at his best when most so, he could not hold himself aloof, but let us know that he loved the pretty girl and hated the oily humbug so vehemently that it is only by a great pull on his reins that he keeps himself straight. It is a family party over which he presides and the reader who becomes, as time goes on, one of Trollope's most intimate cronies has a seat at his right hand. Their relation becomes confidential.

All this, of course, complicates what was simple enough in Defoe and Maupassant. There, we were plainly and straight-forwardly asked to believe. Here, we are asked to believe, but to believe through the medium of Trollope's temperament and, thus, a second relationship is set up with Trollope himself which, if it diverts us, distracts us also. The truth is no longer quite so true. The clear cold truth, which seems to lie before us unveiled in *Gulliver's Travels* and *Moll Flanders* and *La Maison Tellier*, is here garnished with a charming embroidery. But it is not from this attractive embellishment of Trollope's personality that the disease comes which in the end proves fatal to the huge, substantial, well buttressed, and authenticated truth of the Barchester novels. Truth itself, however unpleasant, is interesting always. But, unfortunately, the conditions of story-telling are harsh; they demand that scene shall follow scene; that party shall be supported by another party, one parsonage by another parsonage; that all shall be of the same calibre; that the same values shall prevail. If we are told here that the palace was lit by gas, we must be told there that the manor house was faithful to the oil lamp. But what will happen if, in process of solidifying the entire body of his story, the novelist finds himself out of facts or flagging in his invention? Must he then go on? Yes, for the story has to be finished: the intrigue discovered, the guilty punished, the lovers married in the end. The record, therefore, becomes at times merely a chronicle. Truth peters out into a thin-blooded catalogue. Better would it be, we feel, to leave a blank or even to outrage our sense of probability than to stuff the crevices with this makeshift substance: the wrong side of truth is a worn, dull fabric, unsteeped in the waters of imagination and scorched. But the novel has issued her orders; I consist, she says, of two and thirty chapters; and who am I, we seem to hear the sagacious and humble Trollope ask, with his usual good sense, that I should go disobeying the novel? And he manfully provides us with makeshifts.

If, then, we reckon up what we have got from the truth-tellers, we find that it is a world where our attention is always being drawn to things which can be seen, touched, and tasted, so that we get an acute sense of the reality of our physical existence. Having thus established our belief, the truth-tellers at once contrive that its solidity shall be broken before it becomes oppressive by action. Events happen; coincidence complicates the plain story. But their actions are all in keeping one with another and they are extremely careful not to discredit them or alter the emphasis in any way by making their characters other than such people as naturally express themselves to the full in active and adventurous careers. Then, again, they hold the three great powers which dominate fiction – God, Nature, and Man – in stable relation so that we look at a world in proper perspective; where, moreover, things hold good not only here at the moment in front of us but, there, behind that tree or among those unknown people far away in the shadow behind those hills. At the same time, truth-telling implies disagreeableness. It is part of truth – the sting and edge of it. We cannot deny that Swift, Defoe, and Maupassant all convince us that they reach a more profound depth in their ugliness than Trollope in his pleasantness. For this reason, truth-telling easily swerves a little to one side and becomes satiric. It walks beside the fact and apes it, like a shadow which is only a little more humped and angular than the object which casts it. Yet, in its perfect state, when we can believe absolutely, our satisfaction is complete. Then, we can say, though other states may exist which are better or more exalted, there is none that makes this unnecessary, none that supersedes it. But truth-telling carries in its breast a weakness which is apparent in the works of the lesser writers or in the masters themselves when they are exhausted. Truth-telling is liable to degenerate into perfunctory fact-recording, the repetition of the statement that it was on Wednesday that the Vicar held his mother's meeting which was often attended by Mrs Brown and Miss Dobson in their pony carriage, a statement which, as the reader is quick to perceive, has nothing of truth in it but the respectable outside.

At length, then, taking into account the perfunctory fact-recording, the lack of metaphor, the plainness of the language, and the fact that we believe most when the truth is most painful to us, it is not strange that we should become aware of another desire welling up spontaneously and making its way into those cracks which the great monuments of the truth-tellers wear inevitably upon their solid bases. A desire for distance, for music, for shadow, for space, takes hold of us. The dustman has picked up his broken bottle; he has crossed the road; he begins to lose solidity and detail over there in the evening dusk.

The Romantics

'It was a November morning, and the cliffs which overlooked the ocean were hung with thick and heavy mist, when the portals of the ancient and half ruinous tower, in which Lord Ravenswood had spent the last and troubled years of his life, opened, that his mortal remains might pass forward to an abode yet more dreary and lonely.'

No change could be more complete. The dustman has become a Lord; the present has become the past; homely Anglo-Saxon speech has become Latin and many syllabled; instead of pots and pans, gas jets and snug broughams, we have a half-ruinous tower and cliffs, the ocean and November, heavy in mist. This past and this ruin, this lord and this autumn, this ocean and this cliff are as delightful to us as the change from a close room and voices to the night and the open air. The curious softness and remoteness of the *Bride of Lammermoor*, the atmosphere of rusty moorland and splashing waves, the dark and the distance actually seem to be adding themselves to that other more truthful scene which we still hold in mind, and to be giving it completeness. After that storm this peace, after that glare this coolness. The truth-tellers had very little love, it seems, of nature. They used nature almost entirely as an obstacle to overcome or as a background to complete, not aesthetically for contemplation or for any part it might play in the affairs of their characters. The town, after all, was their natural haunt. But let us compare them in more essential qualities: in their treatment of people. There comes towards us a girl tripping lightly and leaning on her father's arm:

> Lucy Ashton's exquisitely beautiful, yet somewhat girlish features, were formed to express peace of mind, serenity, and indifference to the tinsel of worldly pleasure. Her locks, which were of shadowy gold, divided on a brow of exquisite whiteness, like a gleam of broken and pallid sunshine upon a hill of snow. The expression of the countenance was in the last degree gentle, soft, timid and feminine, and seemed rather to shrink from the most casual look of a stranger than to court his admiration.

Nobody could less resemble Moll Flanders or Mrs Proudie. Lucy Ashton is incapable of action or of self-control. The bull runs at her and she sinks to the ground; the thunder peals and she faints. She falters out the strangest little language of cere-mony and politeness, 'O if you be a man, if you be a gentleman assist me to find my father'. One might say that she has no character except the traditional; to her father she is filial; to her lover, modest; to the poor, benevolent. Compared with Moll Flanders, she is a doll with sawdust in her veins and wax in her cheeks. Yet we have read ourselves into the book and grow familiar with its proportions. We come, at length, to see that anything more individual or eccentric or marked would lay emphasis where we want none. This tapering wraith hovers over the landscape and is part of it. She and Edgar Ravenswood are needed to support this romantic world with their bare forms, to clasp it round with that theme of unhappy love which is needed to hold the rest together. But the world that they clasp has its own laws. It leaves out and eliminates no less drastically than the other. On the one hand, we have feelings of the utmost exaltation – love, hate, jealousy, remorse; on the other hand, raciness and simplicity in the extreme. The rhetoric of the Ashtons and Ravenswoods is completed by the humours of peasants and cackle of village women. The true romantic can swing us from earth to sky; and the great master of romantic fiction, who is undoubtedly Sir Walter Scott, uses his liberty to the full. At the same time, we retort upon this melancholy which he has called forth, as in the *Bride of Lammermoor*. We laugh at ourselves for having been so moved by machinery so absurd. However, before we impute this defect to romance itself, we must consider whether it is not Scott's fault. This lazy-minded man was quite capable when the cold fit was on him of filling a chapter or two currently, conventionally, from a fountain of empty, journalistic phrases which, for all that they have a charm of their own, let the slackened attention sag still further.

Carelessness has never been laid to the charge of Robert Louis Stevenson. He was careful, careful to a fault – a man who combined most strangely boy's psychology with the extreme sophistication of an artist. Yet, he obeyed no less implicitly than Walter Scott the laws of romance. He lays his scene in the past; he is always putting his characters to the sword's point with some desperate adventure; he caps his tragedy with homespun humour. Nor can there be any doubt that his conscience and his seriousness as a writer have stood him in good stead. Take any page of *The Master of Ballantrae* and it still stands wear and tear; but the fabric of the *Bride of Lammermoor* is full of holes and patches; it is scamped, botched, hastily flung together. Here, in Stevenson, romance is treated seriously and given all the advantages of the most refined literary art, with the result that we are never left to consider what an absurd situation this is or to reflect that we have no emotion left with which to meet the demand made upon us. We get, on the contrary, a firm, credible story, which never betrays us for a second, but is corroborated, substantiated, made good in every detail. With what precision and cunning a scene will be made visible to us as if the pen were a knife which sliced away the covering and left the core bare!

'It was as he said: there was no breath stirring; a windless stricture of frost had bound the air; and as we went forth in the shine of the candles, the blackness was like a roof over our heads.' Or, again: 'All the 27th that rigorous weather endured; a stifling cold; folk passing about like smoking chimneys; the wide hearth in the hall piled high with fuel; some of the spring birds that had already blundered north into our neighbourhood besieging the windows of the house or trotting on the frozen turf like things distracted.'

'A windless stricture of frost... folk passing about like smoking chimneys' – one may search the Waverley Novels in vain for such close writing as this. Separately, these descriptions are lovely and brilliant. The fault lies elsewhere, in the whole of which they are a part. For in those critical minutes which decide a book's fate, when it is finished and the book swims up complete in the mind and lets us look at it, something seems lacking. Perhaps it is that the detail sticks out too prominently.

The mind is caught up by this fine passage of description, by that curious exactitude of phrase; but the rhythm and sweep of emotion which the story has started in us are denied satisfaction. We are plucked back when we should be swinging free. Our attention is caught by some knot of ribbon or refinement of tracery when in fact we desire only a bare body against the sky.

Scott repels our taste in a thousand ways. But the crisis, that is the point where the accent falls and shapes the book under it, is right. Slouching, careless as he is, he will at the critical moment pull himself together and strike the one stroke needed, the stroke which gives the book its vividness in memory. Lucy sits gibbering 'couched like a hare upon its form'. 'So, you have ta'en up your bonnie bridegroom?' she says, dropping her fine lady's mincing speech for the vernacular. Ravenswood sinks beneath the quicksands. 'One only vestige of his fate appeared. A large sable feather had been detached from his hat, and the rippling waves of the rising tide wafted it to Caleb's feet. The old man took it up, dried it, and placed it in his bosom.' At both these points the writer's hand is on the book and it falls from him shaped. But in *The Master of Ballantrae*, though each detail is right and wrought so as separately to move our highest admiration, there is no such final consummation. What should have gone to help it seems, in retrospect, to stand apart from it. We remember the detail, but not the whole. Lord Durisdeer and the Master die together but we scarcely notice it. Our attention has been frittered away elsewhere.

It would seem that the romantic spirit is an exacting one; if it sees a man crossing the road in the lamplight and then lost in the gloom of the evening, it at once dictates what course the writer must pursue. We do not wish, it will say, to know much about him. We desire that he shall express our capacity for being noble and adventurous; that he shall dwell among wild places and suffer the extremes of fortune; that he be endowed with youth and distinction and allied with moors, winds, and wild birds. He is, moreover, to be a lover, not in a minute, introspective way, but largely and in outline. His feelings must be part of the landscape; the shallow browns and blues of distant woods and harvest fields are to enter into them; a tower, perhaps, and a castle where the snapdragon flowers. Above all, the romantic spirit demands here a crisis and there a crisis in which the wave that has swollen in the breast shall break. Such feelings Scott gratifies more completely than Stevenson, though with enough qualification to make us pursue the question of romance and its scope and its limitations a little further. Perhaps here it might be interesting to read *The Mysteries of Udolpho*.

The Mysteries of Udolpho have been so much laughed at as the type of Gothic absurdity that it is difficult to come at the book with a fresh eye. We come, expecting to ridicule. Then, when we find beauty; as we do, we go to the other extreme and rhapsodize. But the beauty and the absurdity of romance are both present and the book is a good test of the romantic attitude, since Mrs Radcliffe pushes the liberties of romance to the extreme. Where Scott will go back a hundred years to get the effect of distance, Mrs Radcliffe will go back three hundred. With one stroke, she frees herself from a host of disagreeables and enjoys her freedom lavishly.

As a novelist, it is her desire to describe scenery and it is there that her great gift lies. Like every true writer, she shoulders her way past every obstacle to her goal. She brings us into a huge, empty, airy world. A few ladies and gentlemen, who are purely eighteenth century in mind, manner, and speech, wander about in vast champaigns, listen to nightingales singing amorously in midnight woods; see the sun set over the lagoon of Venice; and watch the distant Alps turn pink and blue from the turrets of an Italian castle. These people, when they are well born, are of the same blood as Scott's gentry; attenuated and formal silhouettes who have the same curious power of being in themselves negligible and insipid but of merging harmoniously in the design.

Again, we feel the force which the romantic acquires by obliterating facts. With the sinking of the lights, the solidity of the foreground disappears, other shapes become apparent and other senses are roused. We become aware of the danger and darkness of our existence; comfortable reality has proved itself a phantom too. Outside our little shelter we hear the wind raging and the waves breaking. In this mood our senses are strained and apprehensive. Noises are audible which we should not hear normally. Curtains rustle. Something in the semi-darkness seems to move. Is it alive? And what is it? And what is it seeking here? Mrs Radcliffe succeeds in making us feel all this, largely because she is able to make us aware of the landscape and, thus, induces a detached mood favourable to romance; but in her, more plainly than in Scott or Stevenson, the absurdity is evident, the wheels of the machine are visible and the grinding is heard. She lets us see more clearly than they do what demands the romantic writer makes upon us.

Both Scott and Stevenson, with the true instinct of the imagination, introduced rustic comedy and broad Scots dialect. It is in that direction, as they rightly divined, that the mind will unbend when it relaxes. Mrs Radcliffe, on the other hand, having climbed to the top of her pinnacle, finds it impossible to come down. She tries to solace us with comic passages, put naturally into the mouths of Annette and Ludovico who are servants. But the break is too steep for her limited and ladylike mind and she pieces out her high moments and her beautiful atmosphere with a pale reflection of romance which is more tedious than any ribaldry. Mysteries abound. Murdered bodies multiply; but she is incapable of creating the emotion to feel them by, with the result that they lie there, unbelieved in; hence, ridiculous. The veil is drawn; there is the concealed figure; there is the decayed face; there are the writhing worms – and we laugh.

Directly the power which lives in a book sinks, the whole fabric of the book, its sentences, the length and shape of them, its inflections, its mannerisms, all that it wore proudly and naturally under the impulse of a true emotion become stale, forced, unappetizing. Mrs Radcliffe slips limply into the faded Scott manner and reels off page after page in a style illustrated by this example:

Emily, who had always endeavoured to regulate her conduct by the nicest laws, and whose mind was finely sensible, not only of what is just in morals, but of whatever is beautiful in the feminine character, was shocked by these words.

And so it slips along and so we sink and drown in the pale tide. Nevertheless, Udolpho passes this test: it gives us an emotion which is both distinct and unique, however high or low we rate the emotion itself.

If we see now where the danger of romance lies: how difficult the mood is to sustain; how it needs the relief of comedy; how the very distance from common human experience and strangeness of its elements become ridiculous – if we see these things, we see also that these emotions are in themselves priceless jewels. The romantic novel realizes for us an emotion which is deep and genuine. Scott, Stevenson, Mrs Radcliffe, all in their different ways, unveil another country of the land of fiction; and it is not the least proof of their power that they breed in us a keen desire for something different.

The Character-Mongers and Comedians

The novels which make us live imaginatively, with the whole of the body as well as the mind, produce in us the physical sensations of heat and cold, noise and silence, one reason perhaps why we desire change and why our reactions to them vary so much at different times. Only, of course, the change must not be violent. It is rather that we need a new scene; a return to human faces; a sense of walls and towns about us, with their lights and their characters after the silence of the wind-blown heath.

After reading the romances of Scott and Stevenson and Mrs Radcliffe, our eyes seem stretched, their sight a little blurred, as if they had been gazing into the distance and it would be a relief to turn for contrast to a strongly marked human face, to characters of extravagant force and character in keeping with our romantic mood. Such figures are most easily to be found in Dickens, of course, and particularly in *Bleak House* where, as Dickens said, 'I have purposely dwelt upon the romantic side of familiar things'. They are found there with peculiar aptness – for if the characters satisfy us by their eccentricity and vigour, London and the landscape of the Dedlocks' place at Chesney Wold are in the mood of the moor, only more luridly lit up and more sharply dark and bright because in Dickens the character-making power is so prodigious that the very houses and streets and fields are strongly featured in sympathy with the people. The character-making power is so prodigious, indeed, that it has little need to make use of observation, and a great part of the delight of Dickens lies in the sense we have of wantoning with human beings twice or ten times their natural size or smallness who retain only enough human likeness to make us refer their feelings very broadly, not to our own, but to those of odd figures seen casually through the half-opened doors of public houses, lounging on quays, slinking mysteriously down little alleys which lie about Holborn and the Law Courts. We enter at once into the spirit of exaggeration.

Who, in the course of a long life, has met Mr Chadband or Mr Turveydrop or Miss Flight? Who has met anybody who, whatever the day or the occasion, can be trusted to say the same phrase, to repeat the same action? This perpetual repetition has, of course, an enormous power to drive these characters home, to stabilize them. Mr Vholes, with his three dear girls at home and his father to support in the Vale of Taunton, Mrs

Jellyby and the natives of Borrioboola-Gha, Mr Turveydrop and his deportment, all serve as stationary points in the flow and confusion of the narrative; they have a decorative effect as if they were gargoyles carved, motionless, at the corner of a composition. Wherever we may have wandered, we shall come back and find them there. They uphold the extraordinary intricacy of the plot in whose confusion we are often sunk up to our lips. For it is impossible to imagine that the Jellybys and the Turveydrops are ever affected by human emotions or that their habitual routine is disturbed by the astonishing events which blow through the pages of the book, from so many quarters at the same time. Thus they have a force, a sublimity, which the slighter and more idiosyncratic characters miss.

After all, is not life itself, with its coincidences and its convolutions, astonishingly queer? 'What connexion,' Dickens himself exclaims, 'can there have been between many people in the innumerable histories of this world, who, from opposite sides of great gulfs, have, nevertheless, been very curiously brought together!' One after another his characters come into being, called into existence by an eye which has only to glance into a room to take in every object, human or inanimate, that is there; by an eye which sees once and for all; which snatches at a woman's steel haircurlers, a pair of red-rimmed eyes, a white scar and makes them somehow reveal the essence of a character; an eye gluttonous, restless, insatiable, creating more than it can use. Thus, the prevailing impression is one of movement, of the endless ebb and flow of life round one or two stationary points.

Often we cease to worry about the plot and wander off down some strange avenue of suggestion, stirred in this vast and mobile world by a casual movement, a word, a glance. 'Still, very steadfastly and quietly walking towards it, a peaceful fig-ure, too, in the landscape, went Mademoiselle Hortense, shoe-less, through the wet grass.' She goes and she leaves a strange wake of emotion behind her. Or, again, a door is flung open in the misty purlieus of London; there is Mr Tulkinghorn's friend, who appears once and once only – 'a man of the same mould and a lawyer too, who lived the same kind of life until he was seventy-five years old, and then, suddenly conceiving (as it is supposed) an impression that it was too monotonous, gave his gold watch to his hairdresser one summer evening, and walked leisurely home to the Temple, and hanged himself'.

This sense that the meaning goes on after the words are spoken, that doors open and let us look through them, is full of romance. But romance in Dickens is impressed on us through characters, through extreme types of human beings, not through castles or banners, not through the violence of action, adventure, or nature. Human faces, scowling, grinning, malignant, benevolent, are projected at us from every corner. Everything is unmitigated and extreme.

But at last, among all these characters who are so static and so extreme, we come upon one – Inspector Bucket, the detective – which is not, as the others are, of a piece, but made up of contrasts and discrepancies. The romantic power of the single-piece character is lost. For the character is no longer fixed and part of the design; it is in itself of interest. Its movements and changes compel us to watch it. We try to understand this many-sided man who has brushed his hair, which is thin, with a wet brush; who has his bombastic, official side, yet with it combines, as we see when the mine is sprung, ability, conscience, even compassion – for all these qualities are displayed by turns in the astonishingly vivid account of the drive through the night and the storm, in pursuit of Esther's mother. If much more were added, so that Inspector Bucket drew more of our attention to him and diverted it from the story, we should begin with his new scale of values in our eyes to find the glaring opposites in use elsewhere too violent to be tolerable. But Dickens committed no such sin against his readers. He uses this clear-cut, many-faced figure to sharpen his final scenes and, then, letting Inspector Bucket of the detective force disappear, gathers the loose folds of the story into one prodigious armful and makes an end. But he has sharpened our curiosity and made us dissatisfied with the limitations and even with the exuberance of his genius. The scene becomes too elastic, too voluminous, too cloud-like in its contours. The very abundance of it tires us, as well as the impossibility of holding it all together. We are always straying down bypaths and into alleys where we lose our way and cannot remember where we were going.

Though the heart of Dickens burned with indignation for public wrongs, he lacked sensitiveness privately, so that his attempts at intimacy failed. His great figures are on too large a scale to fit nicely into each other. They do not interlock. They need company to show them off and action to bring out their humours. They are often out of touch with each other. In Tolstoy, in the scenes between Princess Marya and her father, the old Prince, the pressure of character upon character is never relaxed. The tension is perpetual, every nerve in the character is alive. It may be for this reason that Tolstoy is the greatest of novelists. In Dickens the characters are impressive in themselves but not in their personal relations. Often, indeed, when they talk to each other they are vapid in the extreme or sentimental beyond belief. One thinks of them as independent, existing forever, unchanged, like monoliths looking up into the sky. So it is that we begin to want something smaller, more intense, more intricate. Dickens has, himself, given us a taste of the pleasure we derive from looking curiously and intently into another character. He has made us instinctively reduce the size of the scene in proportion to the figure of a normal man, and now we seek this intensification, this reduction, carried out more perfectly and more completely, we shall find, in the novels of Jane Austen.

At once, when we open *Pride and Prejudice*, we are aware that the sentence has taken on a different character. Dickens, of course, at full stride is as free-paced and far-stretched as possible. But in comparison with this nervous style, how large-limbed and how loose. The sentence here runs like a knife, in and out, cutting a shape clear. It is done in a drawing-room. It is done by the use of dialogue. Half a dozen people come together after dinner and begin, as they so well might, to discuss letter-writing. Mr Darcy writes slowly and 'studies too much for words of four syllables'. Mr Bingley, on the other hand (for it is necessary that we should get to know them both and they can be quickest shown if they are opposed) 'leaves out half his words and blots the rest'. But such is only the first rough shaping that gives the outline of the face. We go on to define and distinguish. Bingley, says Darcy, is really boasting, when he calls himself a careless letter-writer because he thinks the defect interesting. It was a boast when he told Mrs Bennet that if he left Netherfield he would be gone in five minutes. And this little passage of analysis on Darcy's part, besides proving his astuteness and his cool observant temper, rouses Bingley to show us a vivacious picture of Darcy at home. 'I don't know a more awful object than Darcy, on particular occasions, and in particular places; at his own house especially, and of a Sunday evening, when he has nothing to do.'

So, by means of perfectly natural question and answer, everyone is defined and, as they talk, they become not only more clearly seen, but each stroke of the dialogue brings them together or moves them apart, so that the group is no longer casual but interlocked. The talk is not mere talk; it has an emotional intensity which gives it more than brilliance. Light, landscape – everything that lies outside the drawing-room is arranged to illumine it. Distances are made exact; arrangements accurate. It is one mile from Meryton; it is Sunday and not Monday. We want all suspicions and questions laid at rest. It is necessary that the characters should lie before us in as clear and quiet a light as possible since every flicker and tremor is to be observed. Nothing happens, as things so often happen in Dickens, for its own oddity or curiosity but with relation to something else. No avenues of suggestion are opened up, no doors are suddenly flung wide; the ropes which tighten the structure, since they are all rooted in the heart, are so held firmly and tightly. For, in order to develop personal relations to the utmost, it is important to keep out of the range of the abstract, the impersonal; and to suggest that there is anything that lies outside men and women would be to cast the shadow of doubt upon the comedy of their relationships and its sufficiency. So with edged phrases where often one word, set against the current of the phrase, serves to fledge it (thus: 'and whenever any of the cottagers were disposed to be quarrelsome, discontented, or *too poor*') we go down to the depths, for deep they are, for all their clarity.

But personal relations have limits, as Jane Austen seems to realize by stressing their comedy. Everything, she seems to say, has, if we could discover it, a reasonable summing up; and it is extremely amusing and interesting to see the efforts of people to upset the reasonable order, defeated as they invariably are. But if, complaining of the lack of poetry or the lack of tragedy, we are about to frame the familiar statement that this is a world which is too small to satisfy us, a prosaic world, a world of inches and blades of grass, we are brought to a pause by another impression which requires a moment further of analysis. Among all the elements which play upon us in reading fiction there has always been, though in different degrees, some voice, accent, or temperament clearly heard, though behind the scenes of the book. 'Trollope, the novelist, a big, blustering, spectacled, loud-voiced, hunting man'; Scott, the ruined country gentleman, whose very pigs trotted after him, so gracious was the sound of his voice – both come to us with the gesture of hosts, welcoming us, and we fall under the spell of their charm or the interest of their characters.

We cannot say this of Jane Austen, and her absence has the effect of making us detached from her work and of giving it, for all its sparkle and animation, a certain aloofness and completeness. Her genius compelled her to absent herself. So truthful, so clear, so sane a vision would not tolerate distraction, even if it came from her own claims, nor allow the actual experience of a transitory woman to colour what should be unstained by personality. For this reason, then, though we may be less swayed by her, we are less dissatisfied. It may be the very idiosyncrasy of a writer that tires us of him. Jane Austen, who has so little that is peculiar, does not tire us, nor does she breed in us a desire for those writers whose method and style differ altogether from hers. Thus, instead of being urged as the last page is finished to start in search of something that contrasts and completes, we pause when we have read *Pride and Prejudice*.

The pause is the result of a satisfaction which turns our minds back upon what we have just read, rather than forward to something fresh. Satisfaction is, by its nature, removed from analysis, for the quality which satisfies us is the sum of many different parts, so that if we begin praising *Pride and Prejudice* for the qualities that compose it – its wit, its truth, its profound comic power – we shall still not praise it for the quality which is the sum of all these. At this point, then, the mind, brought to bay, escapes the dilemma and has recourse to images. We compare *Pride and Prejudice* to something else because, since satisfaction can be defined no further, all the mind can do is to make a likeness of the thing, and, by giving it another shape, cherish the illusion that it is explaining it, whereas it is, in fact, only looking at it afresh. To say that *Pride and Prejudice* is like a shell, a gem, a crystal, whatever image we may choose, is to see the same thing under a different guise. Yet, perhaps, if we compare *Pride and Prejudice* to something concrete, it is because we are trying to express the sense we have in other novels imperfectly, here with distinctness, of a quality which is not in the story but above it, not in the things themselves but in their arrangement.

Pride and Prejudice, one says, has form; *Bleak House* has not. The eye (so active always in fiction) gives its own interpretation of impressions that the mind has been receiving in different terms. The mind has been conscious in *Pride and Prejudice* that things are said, for all their naturalness, with a purpose; one emotion has been contrasted with another; one scene has been short, the next long; so that all the time, instead of reading at random, without control, snatching at this and that, stressing one thing or another, as the mood takes us, we have been aware of check and stimulus, of spectral architecture built up behind the animation and variety of the scene. It is a quality so precise it is not to be found either in what is said or in what is done; that is, it escapes analysis. It is a quality, too, that is much at the mercy of fiction. Its control is invariably weak there, much weaker than in poetry or in drama because fiction runs so close to life the two are always coming into collison. That this architectural quality can be possessed by a novelist, Jane Austen proves. And she proves, too, that far from chilling the interest or withdrawing the attention from the characters, it seems on the contrary to focus it and add an extra pleasure to the book, a significance. It makes it seem that here is something good in itself, quite apart from our personal feelings.

Not to seek contrast but to start afresh – this is the impulse which urges us on after finishing *Pride and Prejudice*. We must make a fresh start altogether. Personal relations, we recall, have limits. In order to keep their edges sharp, the mysterious, the unknown, the accidental, the strange subside; their intervention would be confusing and distressing. The writer adopts an ironic attitude to her creatures, because she has denied them so many adventures and experiences. A suitable marriage is, after all, the upshot of all this coming together and drawing apart. A world which so often ends in a suitable marriage is not a world to wring one's hands over. On the contrary, it is a world about which we can be sarcastic; into which we can peer endlessly, as we fit the jagged pieces one into another. Thus, it is possible to ask not that her world shall be improved or altered (that our satisfaction forbids) but that another shall be struck off, whose constitution shall be different and shall allow of the other relations. People's relations shall be with God or nature. They shall think. They shall sit, like Dorothea Casaubon in *Middlemarch*, drawing plans for other people's houses; they shall suffer like Gissing's characters in solitude; they shall be alone. *Pride and Prejudice*, because it has such integrity of its own, never for an instant encroaches on other provinces, and, thus, leaves them more clearly defined.

Nothing could be more complete than the difference between *Pride and Prejudice* and *Silas Marner*. Between us and the scene which was so near, so distinct, is now cast a shadow. Something intervenes. The character of Silas Marner is removed from us. It is held in relation to other men and his life compared with human life. This comparison is perpetually made and illustrated by somebody not implicit in the book but inside it, somebody who at once reveals herself as 'I', so that there can be no doubt from the first that we are not going to get the relations of people together, but the spectacle of life so far as 'I' can show it to us. 'I' will do my best to illumine these particular examples of men and women with all the knowledge, all the reflections that, 'I' can offer you.

'I', we at once perceive, has access to many more experiences and reflections than can have come the way of the rustics themselves. She discovers what a simple weaver's emotions on leaving his native village are, by comparing them with those of other people. 'People whose lives have been made various by learning, sometimes find it hard to keep a fast hold on their habitual views of life, on their faith in the Invisible....' It is the observer speaking and we are at once in communication with a grave mind – a mind which it is part of our business to understand. This, of course, darkens and thickens the atmosphere, for we see through so many temperaments; so many side-lights from knowledge, from reflection, play upon what we see; often, even as we are watching the weaver, our minds circle round him and we observe him with an amusement, compassion, or interest which it is impossible that he should feel himself.

Raveloe is not simply a town like Meryton now in existence with certain shops and assembly room; it has a past and therefore the present becomes fleeting, and we enjoy, among other things, the feeling that this is a world in process of change and decay, whose charm is due partly to the fact that it is past. Perhaps we compare it in our own minds with the England of to-day and the Napoleonic wars with those of our own time. All this, if it serves to enlarge the horizon, also makes the village and the people in it who are placed against so wide a view smaller and their impact on each other less sharp. The novelist who believes that personal relations are enough, intensifies them and sharpens them and devotes his power to their investigation. But if the end of life is not to meet, to part, to love, to laugh, if we are at the mercy of other forces, some of them unknown, all of them beyond our power, the urgency of these meetings and partings is blurred and lessened. The edges of the coming together are blunted and the comedy tends to widen itself into a larger sphere and so to modulate into something melancholy, tolerant, and perhaps resigned. George Eliot has removed herself too far from her characters to dissect them keenly or finely, but she has gained the use of her own mind upon these same characters. Jane Austen went in and out of her people's minds like the blood in their veins.

George Eliot has kept the engine of her clumsy and powerful mind at her own disposal. She can use it, when she has created enough matter to use it upon, freely. She can stop at any moment to reason out the motives of the mind that has created it. When Silas Marner discovers that his gold has been stolen, he has recourse to 'that sort of refuge which always comes with the prostration of thought under an overpowering passion; it was that expectation of impossibilities, that belief in contradictory images, which is still distinct from madness, because it is capable of being dissipated by the external fact'. Such analysis is unthinkable in Dickens or in Jane Austen. But it adds something to the character which the character lacked before. It makes us feel not only that the working of the mind is interesting but that we shall get a much truer and subtler understanding of what is actually said and done if we so observe it.

We shall perceive that often an action has only a slight relation to a feeling and, thus, that the truth-tellers, who are content to record accurately what is said and done are often ludicrously deceived and out in their estimate. In other directions there are changes. The use of dialogue is limited; for people can say very little directly. Much more can be said for them or about them by the writer himself. Then, the writer's mind, his knowledge, his skill, not merely the colour of his temperament, become means for bringing out the disposition of the character and also for relating it to other times and places. There is thus revealed underneath a state of mind which often runs counter to the action and the speech.

It is in this direction that George Eliot turns her characters and her scenes. Shadows checker them. All sorts of influences of history, or time, or reflection play upon them. If we consult our own difficult and mixed emotions as we read, it becomes clear that we are fast moving out of the range of pure character-mongering, of comedy, into a far more dubious region.

The Psychologists

Indeed, we have a strange sense of having left every world when we take up *What Maisie Knew*; of being without some support which, even if it impeded us in Dickens and George Eliot, upheld us and controlled us. The visual sense which has hitherto been so active, perpetually sketching fields and farm-houses and faces, seems now to fail or to use its powers to illumine the mind within rather than the world without. Henry James has to find an equivalent for the processes of the mind, to make concrete a mental state. He says, she was 'a ready vessel for bitterness, a deep little porcelain cup in which biting acids could be mixed'. He is forever using this intellectual imagery. The usual supports, the props and struts of the conventions, expressed or observed by the writer, are removed. Everything seems aloof from interference, thrown open to discussion and light, though resting on no visible support. For the minds of which this world is composed seem oddly freed from the pressure of the old encumbrances and raised above the stress of circumstances.

Crises cannot be precipitated by any of the old devices which Dickens and George Eliot used. Murders, rapes, seductions, sudden deaths have no power over this high, aloof world. Here the people are the sport only of delicate influences: of thoughts that people think, but hardly state, about each other; of judgments which people whose time is unoccupied have leisure to devise and apply. In consequence, these characters seem held in a vacuum at a great move from the substantial, lumbering worlds of Dickens and George Eliot or from the precise crisscross of convention which metes out the world of Jane Austen. They live in a cocoon, spun from the finest shades of meaning, which a society, completely unoccupied by the business of getting its living, has time to spin round and about itself. Hence, we are at once conscious of using faculties hitherto dormant, ingenuity and skill, a mental nimbleness and dexterity such as serve to solve a puzzle ingeniously; our pleasure becomes split up, refined, its substance infinitely divided instead of being served to us in one lump.

Maisie, the little girl who is the bone of contention between two parents, each of them claiming her for six months, each of them finally marrying a second husband or wife, lies sunk beneath the depths of suggestion, hint, and conjecture, so that she can only affect us very indirectly, each feeling of hers being deflected and reaching us after glancing off the mind of some other person. Therefore she rouses in us no simple and direct emotion. We always have time to watch it coming and to calculate its pathway, now to the right, now to the left. Cool, amused, intrigued, at every second trying to refine our senses still further and to marshal all that we have of sophisticated intelligence into one section of ourselves, we hang suspended over this aloof little world and watch with intellectual curiosity for the event.

In spite of the fact that our pleasure is less direct, less the result of feeling strongly in sympathy with some pleasure or sorrow, it has a fineness, a sweetness, which the more direct writers fail to give us. This comes in part from the fact that a thousand emotional veins and streaks are perceptible in this twilight or dawn which are lost in the full light of midday.

Besides this fineness and sweetness we get another pleasure which comes when the mind is freed from the perpetual demand of the novelist that we shall feel with his characters. By cutting off the responses which are called out in actual life, the novelist frees us to take delight, as we do when ill or travelling, in things in themselves. We can see the strangeness of them only when habit has ceased to immerse us in them, and we stand outside watching what has no power over us one way or the other. Then we see the mind at work; we are amused by its power to make patterns; by its power to bring out relations in things and disparities which are covered over when we are acting by habit or driven on by the ordinary impulses. It is a pleasure somewhat akin, perhaps, to the pleasure of mathematics or the pleasure of music. Only, of course, since the novelist is using men and women as his subjects, he is perpetually exciting feelings which are opposed to the impersonality of numbers and sound; he seems, in fact, to ignore and to repress their natural feelings, to be coercing them into a plan which we call with vague resentment 'artificial' though it is probable that we are not so foolish as to resent artifice in art. Either through a feeling of timidity or prudery or through a lack of imaginative audacity, Henry James diminishes the interest and importance of his subject in order to bring about a symmetry which is dear to him. This his readers resent. We feel him there, as the suave showman, skilfully manipulating his characters; nipping, repressing; dexterously evading and ignoring, where a writer of greater depth or natural spirits would have taken the risk which his material imposes, let his sails blow full and so, perhaps, achieved symmetry and pattern, in themselves so delightful, all the same.

But it is the measure of Henry James's greatness that he has given us so definite a world, so distinct and peculiar a beauty that we cannot rest satisfied but want to experiment further with these extraordinary perceptions, to understand more and more, but to be free from the perpetual tutelage of the author's presence, his arrangements, his anxieties. To gratify this desire, naturally, we turn to the work of Proust, where we find at once an expansion of sympathy so great that it almost defeats its own object. If we are going to become conscious of everything, how shall we realize anything? Yet if Henry James's world, after the worlds of Dickens and George Eliot, seemed without material boundaries, if everything was pervious to thought and susceptible of twenty shades of meaning, here illumination and analysis are carried far beyond those bounds. For one thing, Henry James himself, the American, ill at ease for all his magnificent urbanity in a strange civilization, was an obstacle never perfectly assimilated even by the juices of his own art. Proust, the product of the civilization which he describes, is so porous, so pliable, so perfectly receptive that we realize him only as an envelope, thin but elastic, which stretches wider and wider and serves not to enforce a view but to enclose a world. His whole universe is steeped in the light of intelligence. The commonest object, such as the telephone, loses its simplicity, its solidity, and becomes a part of life and transparent. The commonest actions, such as going up in an elevator or eating cake, instead of being discharged automatically, rake up in their progress a whole series of thoughts, sensations, ideas, memories which were apparently sleeping on the walls of the mind.

What are we to do with it all? we cannot help asking, as these trophies are piled up round us. The mind cannot be content with holding sensation after sensation passively to itself; something must be done with them; their abundance must be shaped.

Yet at first it would seem as if this vitalizing power has become so fertile that it cumbers the way and trips us up, even when we have need to go quickest, by putting some curious object enticingly in our way. We have to stop and look even against our will.

Thus, when his mother calls him to come to his grandmother's deathbed, the author says, "'I was not asleep,' I answered as I awoke'. Then, even in this crisis, he pauses to explain carefully and subtly why at the moment of waking we so often think for a second that we have not been to sleep. The pause, which is all the more marked because the reflection is not made by 'I' himself but is supplied impersonally by the narrator and therefore, from a different angle, lays a great strain upon the mind, stretched by the urgency of the situation to focus itself upon the dying woman in the next room.

Much of the difficulty of reading Proust comes from this content obliquity. In Proust, the accumulation of objects which surround any central point is so vast and they are often so remote, so difficult of approach and of apprehension that this drawing-together process is gradual, tortuous, and the final relation difficult in the extreme. There is so much more to think about them than one had supposed. One's relations are not only with another person but with the weather, food, clothes, smells, with art and religion and science and history and a thousand other influences.

If one begins to analyse consciousness, it will be found that it is stirred by thousands of small, irrelevant ideas stuffed with odds and ends of knowledge. When, therefore, we come to say something so usual as 'I kissed her', we may well have to explain also how a girl jumped over a man in a deck-chair on the beach before we come tortuously and gradually to the difficult process of describing what a kiss means. In any crisis, such as the death of the grandmother or that moment when the Duchess learns as she steps into her carriage that her old friend Swann is fatally ill, the number of emotions that compose each of these scenes is immensely larger, and they are themselves much more incongruous and difficult of relation than any other scene laid before us by a novelist.

Moreover, if we ask for help in finding our way, it does not come through any of the usual channels. We are never told, as the English novelists so frequently tell us, that one way is right and the other wrong. Every way is thrown open without reserve and without prejudice. Everything that can be felt can be said. The mind of Proust lies open with the sympathy of a poet and the detachment of a scientist to everything that it has the power to feel. Direction or emphasis, to be told that that is right, to be nudged and bidden to attend to that, would fall like a shadow on this profound luminosity and cut off some section of it from our view. The common stuff of the book is made of this deep reservoir of perception. It is from these depths that his characters rise, like waves forming, then break and sink again into the moving sea of thought and comment and analysis which gave them birth.

In retrospect, thus, though as dominant as any characters in fiction, the characters of Proust seem made of a different substance. Thoughts, dreams, knowledge are part of them. They have grown to their full stature, and their actions have met with no rebuff. If we look for direction to help us put them in their places in the universe, we find it negatively in an absence of direction – perhaps sympathy is of more value than interference, understanding than judgment. As a consequence of the union of the thinker and the poet, often, on the heel of some fanatically precise observation, we come upon a flight of imagery – beautiful, coloured, visual, as if the mind, having carried its powers as far as possible in analysis, suddenly rose in the air and from a station high up gave us a different view of the same object in terms of metaphor. This dual vision makes the great characters in Proust and the whole world from which they spring more like a globe, of which one side is always hidden, than a scene laid flat before us, the whole of which we can take in at one glance.

To make this more precise, it might be well to choose another writer, of foreign birth also, who has the same power of illuminating the consciousness from its roots to the surface. Directly we step from the world of Proust to the world of Dostoevsky, we are startled by differences which for a time absorb all our attention. How positive the Russian is, in comparison with the Frenchman. He strikes out a character or a scene by the use of glaring oppositions which are left unbridged. Extreme terms like 'love' and 'hate' are used so lavishly that we must race our imaginations to cover the ground between them. One feels that the mesh of civilization here is made of a coarse netting and the holes are wide apart. Men and women have escaped, compared with the imprisonment that they suffer in Paris. They are free to throw themselves from side to side, to gesticulate, to hiss, to rant, to fall into paroxysms of rage and excitement. They are free, with the freedom that violent emotion gives, from hesitation, from scruple, from analysis. At first we are amazed by the emptiness and the crudity of this world compared with the other. But when we have arranged our perspective a little, it is clear that we are still in the same world – that it is the mind which entices us and the adventures of the mind that concern us. Other worlds, such as Scott's or Defoe's, are incredible. Of this we are assured when we begin to encounter those curious contradictions of which Dostoevsky is so prolific. There is a simplicity in violence which we find nowhere in Proust, but violence also lays bare regions deep down in the mind where contradiction prevails. That contrast which marked Stavrogin's appearance, so that he was at once 'a paragon of beauty, yet at the same time there seemed something repellent about him', is but the crude outer sign of the vice and virtue we meet, at full tilt, in the same breast. The simplification is only on the surface; when the bold and ruthless process, which seems to punch out characters, then to group them together and then to set them all in violent motion, so energetically, so impatiently, is complete, we are shown how, beneath this crude surface, all is chaos and complication. We feel at first that we are in a savage society where the emotions are much simpler and stronger and more impressive than any we encounter in *A la Recherche du Temps perdu*.

Since there are so few conventions, so few barriers (Stavrogin, for instance, passes easily from the depths to the heights of society) the complexity would appear to lie deeper, and these strange contradictions and anomalies which make a man at once divine and bestial would seem to be deep in the heart and not superimposed. Hence, the strange emotional effect of *The Possessed*. It appears to be written by a fanatic ready to sacrifice skill and artifice in order to reveal the soul's difficulties and confusions. The novels of Dostoevsky are pervaded with mysticism; he speaks not as a writer but as a sage, sitting by the roadside in a blanket, with infinite knowledge and infinite patience.

'Yes,' she answered, 'the mother of God is the great mother – the damp earth, and therein lies great joy for men. And every earthly woe and every earthly fear is a joy for us; and when you water the earth with your tears a foot deep, you will rejoice at everything at once, and your sorrow will be no more, such is the prophecy.' That word sank into my heart at the time. Since then when I bow down to the ground at my prayers, I've taken to kissing the earth. I kiss it and weep.

Such is a characteristic passage. But in a novel the voice of the teacher, however exalted, is not enough. We have too many interests to consider, too many problems to face. Consider a scene like that extraordinary party to which Varvara Petrovna has brought Marya, the lame idiot, whom Stavrogin has married 'from a passion for martyrdom, from a craving for remorse, through moral sensuality'. We cannot read to the end without feeling as if a thumb were pressing on a button in us, when we have no emotion left to answer the call. It is a day of surprises, a day of startling revelations, a day of strange coincidences.

For several of the people there (and they come flocking to the room from all quarters) the scene has the greatest emotional importance. Everything is done to suggest the intensity of their emotions. They turn pale; they shake with terror; they go into hysterics. They are thus brought before us in flashes of extreme brilliance – the mad woman with the paper rose in her hat; the young man whose words patter out 'like smooth big grains... One somehow began to imagine that he must have a tongue of special shape, somehow exceptionally long and thin, and extremely red, with a very sharp everlastingly active little tip.'

Yet though they stamp and scream, we hear the sound as if it went on next door. Perhaps the truth is that hate, surprise, anger, horror, are all too strong to be felt continuously. This emptiness and noise lead us to wonder whether the novel of psychology, which projects its drama in the mind, should not, as the truth-tellers showed us, vary and diversify its emotions, lest we shall become numb with exhaustion. To brush aside civilization and plunge into the depths of the soul is not really to enrich. We have, if we turn to Proust, more emotion in a scene which is not supposed to be remarkable, like that in the restaurant in the fog. There we live along a thread of observation which is always going in and out of this mind and that mind; which gathers information from different social levels, which makes us now feel with a prince, now with a restaurant keeper, and brings us into touch with different physical experiences such as light after darkness, safety after danger, so that the imagination is being stimulated on all sides to close slowly, gradually, without being goaded by screams or violence, completely round the object. Proust is determined to bring before the reader every piece of evidence upon which any state of mind is founded; so convinced is Dostoevsky of some point of truth that he sees before him, he will skip and leap to his conclusion with a spontaneity that is in itself stimulating.

By this distortion the psychologist reveals himself. The intellect, which analyses and discriminates, is always and almost at once overpowered by the rush to feeling; whether it is sympathy or anger. Hence, there is something illogical and contradictory often in the characters, perhaps because they are exposed to so much more than the usual current of emotional force. Why does he act like this? we ask again and again, and answer rather doubtfully, that so perhaps madmen act. In Proust, on the other hand, the approach is equally indirect, but it is through what people think and what is thought about them, through the knowledge and thoughts of the author himself, that we come to understand them very slowly and laboriously, but with the whole of our minds.

The books, however, with all these dissimilarities, are alike in this; both are permeated with unhappiness. And this would seem to be inevitable when the mind is not given a direct grasp of whatever it may be. Dickens is in many ways like Dostoevsky; he is prodigiously fertile and he has immense powers of caricature. But Micawber, David Copperfield, and Mrs Gamp are placed directly before us, as if the author saw them from the same angle, and had nothing to do, and no conclusion to draw, except direct amusement or interest. The mind of the author is nothing but a glass between us, or, at most, serves to put a frame round them. All the author's emotional power has gone into them. The surplus of thought and feeling which remained after the characters had been created in George Eliot, to cloud and darken her page, has been used up in the characters of Dickens. Nothing of importance remains over.

But in Proust and Dostoevsky, in Henry James, too, and in all those who set themselves to follow feelings and thoughts, there is always an overflow of emotion from the author as if characters of such subtlety and complexity could be created only when the rest of the book is a deep reservoir of thought and emotion. Thus, though the author himself is not present, characters like Stephen Trofimovitch and Charlus can exist only in a world made of the same stuff as they are, though left unformulated. The effect of this brooding and analysing mind is always to produce an atmosphere of doubt, of questioning, of pain, perhaps of despair. At least, such would seem to be the result of reading *A la Recherche du Temps perdu* and *The Possessed*.

The Satirists and Fantastics

The confused feelings which the psychologists have roused in us, the extraordinary intricacy which they have revealed to us, the network of fine and scarcely intelligible yet profoundly interesting emotions in which they have involved us, set up a craving for relief, at first so primitive that it is almost a physical sensation. The mind feels like a sponge saturated full with sympathy and understanding; it needs to dry itself, to contract upon something hard. Satire and the sense that the satirist gives us that he has the world well within his grasp, so that it is at the mercy of his pen, precisely fulfil our needs.

A further instinct will lead us to pass over such famous satirists as Voltaire and Anatole France in favour of someone writing in our own tongue, writing English. For without any disrespect to the translator we have grown intolerably weary in reading Dostoevsky, as if we were reading with the wrong spectacles or as if a mist had formed between us and the page. We come to feel that every idea is slipping about in a suit badly cut and many sizes too large for it. For a translation makes us understand more clearly than the lectures of any professor the difference between raw words and written words; the nature and importance of what we call style. Even an inferior writer, using his own tongue upon his own ideas, works a change at once which is agreeable and remarkable. Under his pen the sentence shrinks and wraps itself firmly round the meaning, if it be but a little one. The loose, the baggy, shrivels up. And while a writer of passable English will do this, a writer like Peacock does infinitely more.

When we open *Crotchet Castle* and read that first very long sentence which begins, 'In one of those beautiful valleys, through which the Thames (not yet polluted by the tide, the scouring of cities or even the minor defilement of the sandy streams of Surrey)', it would be difficult to describe the relief it gives us, except metaphorically. First there is the shape which recalls something visually delightful, like a flowing wave or the lash of a whip vigorously flung; then as phrase joins phrase and one parenthesis after another pours in its tributary, we have a sense of the whole swimming stream gliding beneath old walls with the shadows of ancient buildings and the glow of green lawns reflected in it. And what is even more delightful after the immensities and obscurities in which we have been living, we are in a world so manageable in scale that we can take its measure, tease it and ridicule it. It is like stepping out into the garden on a perfect September morning when every shadow is sharp and every colour bright after a night of storm and thunder. Nature has submitted to the direction of man. Man himself is dominated by his intelligence. Instead of being many-sided, complicated, elusive, people possess one idiosyncrasy apiece, which crystallizes them into sharp separate characters, colliding briskly when they meet. They seem ridiculously and grotesquely simplified out of all knowledge. Dr Folliott, Mr Firedamp, Mr Skionar, Mr Chainmail, and the rest seem after the tremendous thickness and bulk of the Guermantes and the Stavrogins nothing but agreeable caricatures which a clever old scholar has cut out of a sheet of black paper with a pair of scissors. But on looking closer we find that though it would be absurd to credit Peacock with any desire or perhaps capacity to explore the depths of the soul, his reticence is not empty but suggestive. The character of Dr Folliott is drawn in three strokes of the pen. What lies between is left out. But each stroke indicates the mass behind it, so that the reader can make it out for himself; while it has, because of this apparent simplicity, all the sharpness of a caricature. The world so happily constituted that there is always trout for breakfast, wine in the cellar, and some amusing contretemps, such as the cook setting herself alight and being put out by the footman, to make us laugh – a world where there is nothing more pressing to do than to 'glide over the face of the waters, discussing everything and settling nothing', is not the world of pure fantasy; it is close enough to be a parody of our world and to make our own follies and the solemnities of our institutions look a little silly.

The satirist does not, like the psychologist, labour under the oppression of omniscience. He has leisure to play with his mind freely, ironically. His sympathies are not deeply engaged. His sense of humour is not submerged.

But the prime distinction lies in the changed attitude towards reality. In the psychologists the huge burden of facts is based upon a firm foundation of dinner, luncheon, bed and breakfast. It is with surprise, yet with relief and a start of pleasure, that we accept Peacock's version of the world, which ignores so much, simplifies so much, gives the old globe a spin and shows another face of it on the other side. It is unnecessary to be quite so painstaking, it seems. And, after all, is not this quite as real, as true as the other? And perhaps all this pother about 'reality' is overdone. The great gain is perhaps that our relation with things is more distant. We reap the benefit of a more poetic point of view. A line like the charming 'At Godstow, they gathered hazel on the grave of Rosamond' could be written only by a writer who was at a certain distance from his people, so that there need be no explanations. For certainly with Trollope's people explanations would have been necessary; we should have wanted to know what they had been doing, gathering hazel, and where they had gone for dinner afterwards and how the carriage had met them. 'They', however, being Chainmail, Skionar, and the rest, are at liberty to gather hazel on the grave of Rosamond if they like; as they are free to sing a song if it so pleases them or to debate the march of mind.

The romantic took the same liberty but for another purpose. In the satirist we get not a sense of wildness and the soul's adventures, but that the mind is free and therefore sees through and dispenses with much that is taken seriously by writers of another calibre.

There are, of course, limitations, reminders, even in the midst of our pleasure, of boundaries that we must not pass. We cannot imagine in the first place that the writer of such exquisite sentences can cover many reams of paper; they cost too much to make. Then again a writer who gives us so keen a sense of his own personality by the shape of his phrase is limited. We are always being brought into touch, not with Peacock himself, as with Trollope himself (for there is no giving away of his own secrets; he does not conjure up the very shape of himself and the sound of his laughter as Trollope does), but all the time our thought is taking the colour of his thought, we are insensibly thinking in his measure. If we write, we try to write in his manner, and this brings us into far greater intimacy with him than with writers like Trollope again or Scott, who wrap their thought up quite adequately in a duffle gray blanket which wears well and suits everything. This may in the end, of course, lead to some restriction. Style may carry with it, especially in prose, so much personality that it keeps us within the range of that personality. Peacock pervades his book.

In order that we may consider this more fully let us turn from Peacock to Sterne, a much greater writer, yet sufficiently in the family of Peacock to let us carry on the same train of thought uninterruptedly.

At once we are aware that we are in the presence of a much subtler mind, a mind of far greater reach and intensity. Peacock's sentences, firmly shaped and beautifully polished as they are, cannot stretch as these can. Here our sense of elasticity is increased so much that we scarcely know where we are. We lose our sense of direction. We go backwards instead of forwards. A simple statement starts a digression; we circle; we soar; we turn round; and at last back we come again to Uncle Toby who has been sitting meanwhile in his black plush breeches with his pipe in his hand. Proust, it maybe said, was as tortuous, but his indirectness was due to his immense powers of analysis and to the fact that directly he had made a simple statement he perceived and must make us perceive all that it implied. Sterne is not an analyst of other people's sensations. Those remain simple, eccentric, erratic. It is his own mind that fascinates him, its oddities and its whims, its fancies and its sensibilities; and it is his own mind that colours the book and gives it walls and shape. Yet it is obvious that his claim is just when he says that however widely he may digress, to my Aunt Dinah and the coachman and then 'some millions of miles into the very heart of the planetary system', when he is by way of telling about Uncle Toby's character, still 'the drawing of my Uncle Toby's character went on gently all the time – not the great contours of it – that was impossible – but some familiar strokes and faint designations of it… so that you are much better acquainted with my Uncle Toby now than you were before'. It is true, for we are always alighting as we skim and circle to deposit some little grain of observation upon the figure of Uncle Toby sitting there with his pipe in his hand. There is thus built up intermittently, irregularly, an extraordinary portrait of a character – a character shown most often in a passive state, sitting still, through the quick glancing eyes of an erratic observer, who never lets his character speak more than a few words or take more than a few steps in his proper person, but is forever circling round and playing with the lapels of his coat and peering up into his face and teasing him affectionately, whimsically, as if he were the attendant sprite in charge of some unconscious mortal. Two such opposites were made to show each other off and draw each other out. One relishes the simplicity, the modesty, of Uncle Toby all the more comparing them with the witty, indecent, disagreeable, yet highly sympathetic, character of the author.

All through *Tristram Shandy* we are aware of this blend and contrast. Laurence Sterne is the most important character in the book. It is true that at the critical moment the author obliterates himself and gives his characters that little extra push which frees them from his tutelage so that they are something more than the whims and fancies of a brilliant brain. But since character is largely made up of surroundings and circumstances, these people whose surroundings are so queer, who are often silent themselves but always so whimsically talked about, are a race apart among the people of fiction. There is nothing like them elsewhere, for in no other book are the characters so closely dependent on the author. In no other book are the writer and reader so involved together. So, finally, we get a book in which all the usual conventions are consumed and yet no ruin or catastrophe comes to pass; the whole subsists complete by itself, like a house which is miraculously habitable without the help of walls, staircases, or partitions. We live in the humours, contortions, and oddities of the spirit, not in the slow unrolling of the long length of life. And the reflection comes, as we sun ourselves on one of these high pinnacles, can we not escape even further, so that we are not conscious of any author at all? Can we not find poetry in some novel or other? For Sterne by the beauty of his style has let us pass beyond the range of personality into a world which is not altogether the world of fiction. It is above.

The Poets

Certain phrases have brought about this change in us. They have raised us out of the atmosphere of fiction; they have made us pause to wonder. For instance:

I will not argue the matter; Time wastes too fast: every letter I trace tells me with what rapidity Life follows my pen; the days and hours of it more precious, – my dear Jenny – than the rubies about thy neck, are flying over our heads like light clouds of a windy day, never to return more; everything presses on, – whilst thou art twisting that lock; – see! it grows grey; and every time I kiss thy hand to bid adieu, and every absence which follows it, are preludes to that eternal separation which we are shortly to make.

Phrases like this bring, by the curious rhythm of their phrasing, by a touch on the visual sense, an alteration in the movement of the mind which makes it pause and widen its gaze and slightly change its attention. We are looking out at life in general.

But though Sterne with his extraordinary elasticity could use this effect, too, without incongruity, that is only possible because his genius is rich enough to let him sacrifice some of the qualities that are native to the character of the novel without our feeling it. It is obvious that there is no massing together of the experiences of many lives and many minds as in *War and Peace;* and, too, that there is something of the essayist, something of the soliloquist in the quips and quirks of this brilliant mind. He is sometimes sentimental, as if after so great a display of singularity he must assert his interest in the normal lives and affections of his people. Tears are necessary; tears are pumped up. Be that as it may, exquisite and individual as his poetry is, there is another poetry which is more natural to the novel, because it uses the material which the novelist provides. It is the poetry of situation rather than of language, the poetry which we perceive when Catherine in *Wuthering Heights* pulls the feathers from the pillow; when Natasha in *War and Peace* looks out of the window at the stars. And it is significant that we recall this poetry, not as we recall it in verse, by the words, but by the scene. The prose remains casual and quiet enough so that to quote it is to do little or nothing to explain its effect. Often we have to go far back and read a chapter or more before we can come by the impression of beauty or intensity that possessed us.

Yet it is not to be denied that two of the novelists who are most frequently poetical – Meredith and Hardy – are as novelists imperfect. Both *The Ordeal of Richard Feverel* and *Far from the Madding Crowd* are books of great inequality. In both we feel a lack of control, an incoherence such as we never feel in *War and Peace* or in *A la Recherche du Temps perdu* or in *Pride and Prejudice*. Both Hardy and Meredith are too fully charged, it would seem, with a sense of poetry and have too limited or too imperfect a sympathy with human beings to express it adequately through that channel. Hence, as we so often find in Hardy, the impersonal element – Fate, the Gods, whatever name we choose to call it – dominates the people. They appear wooden, melodramatic, unreal. They cannot express the poetry with which the writer himself is charged through their own lips, for their psychology is inadequate, and thus the expression is left to the writer, who assumes a character apart from his people and cannot return to them with perfect ease when the time comes.

Again, in Meredith the writer's sense of the poetry of youth, of love, of nature is heard like a song to which the characters listen passively without moving a muscle; and then, when the song is done, on they move again with a jerk. This would seem to prove that a profound poetic sense is a dangerous gift for the novelist; for in Hardy and Meredith poetry seems to mean something impersonal, generalized, hostile to the idiosyncrasy of character, so that the two suffer if brought into touch. It may be that the perfect novelist expresses a different sort of poetry, or has the power of expressing it in a manner which is not harmful to the other qualities of the novel. If we recall the passages that have seemed to us, in retrospect at any rate, to be poetical in fiction we remember them as part of the novel. When Natasha in *War and Peace* looks out of the window at the stars, Tolstoy produces a feeling of deep and intense poetry without any disruption or that disquieting sense of song being sung to people who listen. He does this because his poetic sense finds expression in the poetry of the situation or because his characters express it in their own words, which are often of the simplest. We have been living in them and knowing them, so that, when Natasha leans on the window sill and thinks of her life to come, our feelings of the poetry of the moment do not lie in what she says so much as in our sense of her who is saying it.

Wuthering Heights again is steeped in poetry. But here there is a difference, for one can hardly say that the profound poetry of the scene where Catherine pulls the feathers from the pillow has anything to do with our knowledge of her or adds to our understanding or our feeling about her future. Rather it deepens and controls the wild, stormy atmosphere of the whole book. By a master stroke of vision, rarer in prose than in poetry, people and scenery and atmosphere are all in keeping. And, what is still rarer and more impressive, through that atmosphere we seem to catch sight of larger men and women, of other symbols and significances. Yet the characters of Heathcliff and Catherine are perfectly natural; they contain all the poetry that Emily Brontë herself feels without effort. We never feel that this is a poetic moment, apart from the rest, or that here Emily Brontë is speaking to us through her characters. Her emotion has not overflowed and risen up independently, in some comment or attitude of her own. She is using her characters to express her conception, so that her people are active agents in the book's life, adding to its impetus and not impeding it. The same thing happens, more explicitly but with less concentration, in *Moby Dick*. In both books we get a vision of presence outside the human beings, of a meaning that they stand for, without ceasing to be themselves. But it is notable that both Emily Brontë and Herman Melville ignore the greater part of those spoils of the modern spirit which Proust grasps so tenaciously and transforms so triumphantly. Both the earlier writers simplify their characters till only the great contour, the clefts and ridges of the face, are visible. Both seem to have been content with the novel as their form and with prose as their instrument provided that they could remove the scene far from towns, simplify the actors and allow nature at her wildest to take part in the scene. Thus we can say that there is poetry in novels both where the poetry is expressed not so much by the particular character in a particular situation, like Natasha in the window, but rather by the whole mood and temper of the book, like the mood and temper of *Wuthering Heights* or *Moby Dick* to which the characters of Catherine or Heathcliff or Captain Ahab give expression.

In *A la Recherche du Temps perdu*, however, there is as much poetry as in any of these books; but it is poetry of a different kind. The analysis of emotion is carried further by Proust than by any other novelist; and the poetry comes, not in the situation, which is too fretted and voluminous for such an effect, but in those frequent passages of elaborate metaphor, which spring out of the rock of thought like fountains of sweet water and serve as translations from one language into another. It is as though there were two faces to every situation; one full in the light so that it can be described as accurately and examined as minutely as possible; the other half in shadow so that it can be described only in a moment of faith and vision by the use of metaphor. The longer the novelist pores over his analysis, the more he becomes conscious of something that forever escapes. And it is this double vision that makes the work of Proust to us in our generation so spherical, so comprehensive. Thus, while Emily Brontë and Herman Melville turn the novel away from shore out to sea, Proust on the other hand rivets his eyes on men.

And here we may pause, not, certainly, that there are no more books to read or no more changes of mood to satisfy, but for a reason which springs from the youth and vigour of the art itself. We can imagine so many different sorts of novels, we are conscious of so many relations and susceptibilities the novelist had not expressed that we break off in the middle with Emily Brontë or with Tolstoy without any pretence that the phases of fiction are complete or that our desires as a reader have received full satisfaction. On the contrary, reading excites them; they well up and make us inarticulately aware of a dozen different novels that wait just below the horizon unwritten. Hence the futility at present of any theory of 'the future of fiction'. The next ten years will certainly upset it; the next century will blow it to the winds. We have only to remember the comparative youth of the novel, that it is, roughly speaking, about the age of English poetry in the time of Shakespeare, to realize the folly of any summary, or theory of the future of the art. Moreover, prose itself is still in its infancy, and capable, no doubt, of infinite change and development.

But our rapid journey from book to book has left us with some notes made by the way and these we may sort out, not so much to seek a conclusion as to express the brooding, the meditative mood which follows the activity of reading. So then, in the first place, even though the time at our disposal has been short, we have travelled, in reading these few books, a great distance emotionally. We have plodded soberly along the high road talking plain sense and meeting many interesting adventures; turning romantic, we have lived in castles and been hunted on moors and fought gallantly and died; then tired of this, we have come into touch with humanity again, at first romantically prodigiously, enjoying the society of giants and dwarfs, the huge and the deformed, and then again tiring of this extravagance, have reduced them, by means of Jane Austen's microscope, to perfectly proportioned and normal men and women and the chaotic world to English parsonage, shrubberies, and lawns.

But a shadow next falls upon that bright prospect, distorting the lovely harmony of its proportions. The shadow of our own minds has fallen upon it and gradually we have drawn within, and gone exploring with Henry James endless filaments of feeling and relationship in which men and women are enmeshed, and so we have been led on with Dostoevsky to descend miles and miles into the deep and yeasty surges of the soul.

At last Proust brings the light of an immensely civilized and saturated intelligence to bear upon this chaos and reveals the infinite range and complexity of human sensibility. But in following him we lose the sense of outline, and to recover it seek out the satirists and the fantastics, who stand aloof and hold the world at a distance and eliminate and reduce so that we have the satisfaction of seeing round things after being immersed in them. And the satirists and the fantastics, like Peacock and Sterne, because of their detachment, write often as poets write, for the sake of the beauty of the sentence and not for the sake of its use, and so stimulate us to wish for poetry in the novel. Poetry, it would seem, requires a different ordering of the scene; human beings are needed, but needed in their relation to love, or death, or nature rather than to each other. For this reason their psychology is simplified, as it is both in Meredith and Hardy, and instead of feeling the intricacy of life, we feel its passion, its tragedy. In *Wuthering Heights* and in *Moby Dick* this simplification, far from being empty, has greatness, and we feel that something beyond, which is not human yet does not destroy their humanity or the actions. So, briefly, we may sum up our impressions. Brief and fragmentary as they are, we have gained some sense of the vastness of fiction and the width of its range.

As we look back it seems that the novelist can do anything. There is room in a novel for story-telling, for comedy, for tragedy, for criticism and information and philosophy and poetry. Something of its appeal lies in the width of its scope and the satisfaction it offers to so many different moods, desires, and instincts on the part of the reader. But however the novelist may vary his scene and alter the relations of one thing to another – and as we look back we see the whole world in perpetual transformation – one element remains constant in all novels, and that is the human element; they are about people, they excite in us the feelings that people excite in us in real life. The novel is the only form of art which seeks to make us believe that it is giving a full and truthful record of the life of a real person.

And in order to give that full record of life, not the climax and the crisis but the growth and development of feelings, which is the novelist's aim, he copies the order of the day, observes the sequence of ordinary things even if such fidelity entails chapters of description and hours of research. Thus we glide into the novel with far less effort and less break with our surroundings than into any other form of imaginative literature. We seem to be continuing to live, only in another house or country perhaps. Our most habitual and natural sympathies are roused with the first words; we feel them expand and contract, in liking or disliking, hope or fear on every page. We watch the character and behaviour of Becky Sharp or Richard Feverel and instinctively come to an opinion about them as about real people, tacitly accepting this or that impression, judging each motive, and forming the opinion that they are charming but insincere, good or dull, secretive but interesting, as we make up our minds about the characters of the people we meet.

This engaging lack of artifice and the strength of the emotion that he is able to excite are great advantages to the novelist, but they are also great dangers. For it is inevitable that the reader who is invited to live in novels as in life should go on feeling as he feels in life. Novel and life are laid side by side. We want happiness for the character we like, punishment for those we dislike. We have secret sympathies for those who seem to resemble us. It is difficult to admit that the book may have merit if it outrages our sympathies, or describes a life which seems unreal to us. Again we are acutely aware of the novelist's character and speculate upon his life and adventures. These personal standards extend in every direction, for every sort of prejudice, every sort of vanity, can be snubbed or soothed by the novelist. Indeed the enormous growth of the psychological novel in our time has been prompted largely by the mistaken belief, which the reader has imposed upon the novelist, that truth is always good; even when it is the truth of the psychoanalyst and not the truth of imagination.

Such vanities and emotions on the part of the reader are perpetually forcing the novelist to gratify them. And the result, though it may give the novel a short life of extreme vigour, is, as we know even while we are enjoying the tears and laughs and excitement of that life, fatal to its endurance. For the accuracy of representation, the looseness and simplicity of its method, its denial of artifice and convention, its immense power to imitate the surface reality – all the qualities that make a novel the most popular form of literature – also make it, even as we read it, turn stale and perish on our hands. Already some of the 'great novels' of the past, like *Robert Elsmere* or *Uncle Tom's Cabin*, are perished except in patches because they were originally bolstered up with so much that had virtue and vividness only for those who lived at the moment that the books were written. Directly manners change, or the contemporary idiom alters, page after page, chapter after chapter, become obsolete and lifeless.

But the novelist is aware of this too and, while he uses the power of exciting human sympathy which belongs to him, he also attempts to control it. Indeed the first sign that we are reading a writer of merit is that we feel this control at work on us. The barrier between us and the book is raised higher. We do not slip so instinctively and so easily into a world that we know already. We feel that we are being compelled to accept an order and to arrange the elements of the novel – man, nature, God – in certain relations at the novelist's bidding. In looking back at the few novels that we have glanced at here we can see how astonishingly we lend ourselves to first one vision and then to another which is its opposite. We obliterate a whole universe at the command of Defoe; we see every blade of grass and snail shell at the command of Proust. From the first page we feel our minds trained upon a point which becomes more and more perceptible as the book proceeds and the writer brings his conception out of darkness. At last the whole is exposed to view. And then, when the book is finished, we seem to see (it is strange how visual the impression is) something girding it about like the firm road of Defoe's storytelling; or we see it shaped and symmetrical with dome and column complete, like *Pride and Prejudice* and *Emma*. A power which is not the power of accuracy or of humour or of pathos is also used by the great novelists to shape their work. As the pages are turned, something is built up which is not the story itself. And this power, if it accentuates and concentrates and gives the fluidity of the novel endurance and strength, so that no novel can survive even a few years without it, is also a danger. For the most characteristic qualities of the novel – that it registers the slow growth and development of feeling, that it follows many lives and traces their unions and fortunes over a long stretch of time – are the very qualities that are most incompatible with design and order. It is the gift of style, arrangement, construction, to put us at a distance from the special life and to obliterate its features; while it is the gift of the novel to bring us into close touch with life.

The two powers fight if they are brought into combination. The most complete novelist must be the novelist who can balance the two powers so that the one enhances the other.

This would seem to prove that the novel is by its nature doomed to compromise, wedded to mediocrity. Its province, one may conclude, is to deal with the commoner but weaker emotions; to express the bulk and not the essence of life. But any such verdict must be based upon the supposition that 'the novel' has a certain character which is now fixed and cannot be altered, that 'life' has a certain limit which can be defined. And it is precisely this conclusion that the novels we have been reading tend to upset.

The process of discovery goes on perpetually. Always more of life is being reclaimed and recognized. Therefore, to fix the character of the novel, which is the youngest and most vigorous of the arts, at this moment would be like fixing the character of poetry in the eighteenth century and saying that because

Gray's *Elegy* was 'poetry' *Don Juan* was impossible. An art practised by hosts of people, sheltering diverse minds, is also bound to be simmering, volatile, unstable. And for some reason not here to be examined, fiction is the most hospitable of hosts; fiction to-day draws to itself writers who would even yesterday have been poets, dramatists, pamphleteers, historians. Thus 'the novel', as we still call it with such parsimony of language, is clearly splitting apart into books which have nothing in common but this one inadequate title. Already the novelists are so far apart that they scarcely communicate, and to one novelist the work of another is quite genuinely unintelligible or quite genuinely negligible.

The most significant proof of this fertility, however, is provided by our sense of feeling something that has not yet been said; of some desire still unsatisfied. A very general, a very elementary, view of this desire would seem to show that it points in two directions. Life – it is a commonplace – is growing more complex. Our self-consciousness is becoming far more alert and better trained. We are aware of relations and subtleties which have not yet been explored. Of this school Proust is the pioneer, and undoubtedly there are still to be born writers who will carry the analysis of Henry James still further, who will reveal and relate finer threads of feeling, stranger and more obscure imaginations.

But also we desire synthesis. The novel, it is agreed, can follow life; it can amass details. But can it also select? Can it symbolize? Can it give us an epitome as well as an inventory? It was some such function as this that poetry discharged in the past. But, whether for the moment or for some longer time, poetry with her rhythms, her poetic diction, her strong flavour of tradition, is too far from us to-day to do for us what she did for our parents. Prose perhaps is the instrument best fitted to the complexity and difficulty of modern life. And prose – we have to repeat it – is still so youthful that we scarcely know what powers it may not hold concealed within it. Thus it is possible that the novel in time to come may differ as widely from the novel of Tolstoy and Jane Austen as the poetry of Browning and Byron differs from the poetry of Lydgate and Spenser. In time to come – but time to come lies far beyond our province.

Women and Fiction

The Forum, **March 1929**

The title of this article can be read in two ways: it may allude to women and the fiction that they write, or to women and the fiction that is written about them. The ambiguity is intentional, for in dealing with women as writers, as much elasticity as possible is desirable; it is necessary to leave oneself room to deal with other things besides their work, so much has that work been influenced by conditions that have nothing whatever to do with art.

The most superficial inquiry into women's writing instantly raises a host of questions. Why, we ask at once, was there no continuous writing done by women before the eighteenth century? Why did they then write almost as habitually as men, and in the course of that writing produce, one after another, some of the classics of English fiction? And why did their art then, and why to some extent does their art still, take the form of fiction?

A little thought will show us that we are asking questions to which we shall get, as answer, only further fiction. The answer lies at present locked in old diaries, stuffed away in old drawers, half-obliterated in the memories of the aged. It is to be found in the lives of the obscure – in those almost unlit corridors of history where the figures of generations of women are so dimly, so fitfully perceived. For very little is known about women. The history of England is the history of the male line, not of the female. Of our fathers we know always some fact, some distinction. They were soldiers or they were sailors; they filled that office or they made that law. But of our mothers, our grandmothers, our great-grandmothers, what remains? Nothing but a tradition. One was beautiful; one was red-haired; one was kissed by a Queen. We know nothing of them except their names and the dates of their marriages and the number of children they bore.

Thus, if we wish to know why at any particular time women did this or that, why they wrote nothing, why on the other hand they wrote masterpieces, it is extremely difficult to tell. Anyone who should seek among those old papers, who should turn history wrong side out and so construct a faithful picture of the daily life of the ordinary woman in Shakespeare's time, in Milton's time, in Johnson's time, would not only write a book of astonishing interest, but would furnish the critic with a weapon which he now lacks. The extraordinary woman depends on the ordinary woman. It is only when we know what were the conditions of the average woman's life – the number of her children, whether she had money of her own, if she had a room to herself, whether she had help in bringing up her family, if she had servants, whether part of the housework was her task – it is only when we can measure the way of life and the experience of life made possible to the ordinary woman that we can account for the success or failure of the extraordinary woman as a writer.

Strange spaces of silence seem to separate one period of activity from another. There was Sappho and a little group of women all writing poetry on a Greek island six hundred years before the birth of Christ. They fall silent. Then about the year 1000 we find a certain court lady, the Lady Murasaki, writing a very long and beautiful novel in Japan. But in England in the sixteenth century, when the dramatists and poets were most active, the women were dumb. Elizabethan literature is exclusively masculine. Then, at the end of the eighteenth century and in the beginning of the nineteenth, we find women again writing – this time in England – with extraordinary frequency and success.

Law and custom were of course largely responsible for these strange intermissions of silence and speech. When a woman was liable, as she was in the fifteenth century, to be beaten and flung about the room if she did not marry the man of her parents' choice, the spiritual atmosphere was not favourable to the production of works of art. When she was married without her own consent to a man who thereupon became her lord and master, 'so far at least as law and custom could make him', as she was in the time of the Stuarts, it is likely she had little time for writing, and less encouragement. The immense effect of environment and suggestion upon the mind, we in our psychoanalytical age are beginning to realize. Again, with memoirs and letters to help us, we are beginning to understand how abnormal is the effort needed to produce a work of art, and what shelter and what support the mind of the artist requires. Of those facts the lives and letters of men like Keats and Carlyle and Flaubert assure us.

Thus it is clear that the extraordinary outburst of fiction in the beginning of the nineteenth century in England was heralded by innumerable slight changes in law and customs and manners. And women of the nineteenth century had some leisure; they had some education. It was no longer the exception for women of the middle and upper classes to choose their own husbands. And it is significant that of the four great women novelists – Jane Austen, Emily Brontë, Charlotte Brontë, and George Eliot – not one had a child, and two were unmarried.

Yet, though it is clear that the ban upon writing had been removed, there was still, it would seem, considerable pressure upon women to write novels. No four women can have been more unlike in genius and character than these four. Jane Austen can have had nothing in common with George Eliot; George Eliot was the direct opposite of Emily Brontë. Yet all were trained for the same profession; all, when they wrote, wrote novels.

Fiction was, as fiction still is, the easiest thing for a woman to write. Nor is it difficult to find the reason. A novel is the least concentrated form of art. A novel can be taken up or put down more easily than a play or a poem. George Eliot left her work to nurse her father. Charlotte Brontë put down her pen to pick the eyes out of the potatoes. And living as she did in the common sitting-room, surrounded by people, a woman was trained to use her mind in observation and upon the analysis of character. She was trained to be a novelist and not to be a poet.

Even in the nineteenth century, a woman lived almost solely in her home and her emotions. And those nineteenth-century novels, remarkable as they were, were profoundly influenced by the fact that the women who wrote them were excluded by their sex from certain kinds of experience. That experience has a great influence upon fiction is indisputable. The best part of Conrad's novels, for instance, would be destroyed if it had been impossible for him to be a sailor. Take away all that Tolstoi knew of war as a soldier, of life and society as a rich young man whose education admitted him to all sorts of experience, and *War and Peace* would be incredibly impoverished.

Yet *Pride and Prejudice*, *Wuthering Heights*, *Villette*, and *Middlemarch* were written by women from whom was forcibly withheld all experience save that which could be met with in a middle-class drawing-room. No first-hand experience of war or seafaring or politics or business was possible for them. Even their emotional life was strictly regulated by law and custom. When George Eliot ventured to live with Mr Lewes without being his wife, public opinion was scandalized. Under its pressure she withdrew into a suburban seclusion which, inevitably, had the worst possible effects upon her work. She wrote that unless people asked of their own accord to come and see her, she never invited them. At the same time, on the other side of Europe, Tolstoi was living a free life as a soldier, with men and women of all classes, for which nobody censured him and from which his novels drew much of their astonishing breadth and vigour.

But the novels of women were not affected only by the necessarily narrow range of the writer's experience. They showed, at least in the nineteenth century, another characteristic which may be traced to the writer's sex. In *Middlemarch* and in *Jane*

Eyre we are conscious not merely of the writer's character, as we are conscious of the character of Charles Dickens, but we are conscious of a woman's presence – of someone resenting the treatment of her sex and pleading for its rights. This brings into women's writing an element which is entirely absent from a man's, unless, indeed, he happens to be a working-man, a negro, or one who for some other reason is conscious of disability. It introduces a distortion and is frequently the cause of weakness. The desire to plead some personal cause or to make a character the mouthpiece of some personal discontent or grievance always has a distressing effect, as if the spot at which the reader's attention is directed were suddenly twofold instead of single.

The genius of Jane Austen and Emily Brontë is never more convincing than in their power to ignore such claims and solicitations and to hold on their way unperturbed by scorn or censure. But it needed a very serene or a very powerful mind to resist the temptation to anger. The ridicule, the censure, the assurance of inferiority in one form or another which were lavished upon women who practised an art, provoked such reactions naturally enough. One sees the effect in Charlotte Brontë's indignation, in George Eliot's resignation. Again and again one finds it in the work of the lesser women writers – in their choice of a subject, in their unnatural self-assertiveness, in their unnatural docility. Moreover, insincerity leaks in almost unconsciously. They adopt a view in deference to authority. The vision becomes too masculine or it becomes too feminine; it loses its perfect integrity and, with that, its most essential quality as a work of art.

The great change that has crept into women's writing is, it would seem, a change of attitude. The woman writer is no longer bitter. She is no longer angry. She is no longer pleading and protesting as she writes. We are approaching, if we have not yet reached, the time when her writing will have little or no foreign influence to disturb it. She will be able to concentrate upon her vision without distraction from outside. The aloofness that was once within the reach of genius and originality is only now coming within the reach of ordinary women. Therefore the average novel by a woman is far more genuine and far more interesting to-day than it was a hundred or even fifty years ago.

But it is still true that before a woman can write exactly as she wishes to write, she has many difficulties to face. To begin with, there is the technical difficulty – so simple, apparently; in reality, so baffling – that the very form of the sentence does not fit her. It is a sentence made by men; it is too loose, too heavy, too pompous for a woman's use. Yet in a novel, which covers so wide a stretch of ground, an ordinary and usual type of sentence has to be found to carry the reader on easily and naturally from one end of the book to the other. And this a woman must make for herself, altering and adapting the current sentence until she writes one that takes the natural shape of her thought without crushing or distorting it.

But that, after all, is only a means to an end, and the end is still to be reached only when a woman has the courage to surmount opposition and the determination to be true to herself. For a novel, after all, is a statement about a thousand different objects – human, natural, divine; it is an attempt to relate them to each other. In every novel of merit these different elements are held in place by the force of the writer's vision. But they have another order also, which is the order imposed upon them by convention. And as men are the arbiters of that convention, as they have established an order of values in life, so too, since fiction is largely based on life, these values prevail there also to a very great extent.

It is probable, however, that both in life and in art the values of a woman are not the values of a man. Thus, when a woman comes to write a novel, she will find that she is perpetually wishing to alter the established values – to make serious what appears insignificant to a man, and trivial what is to him important. And for that, of course, she will be criticized; for the critic of the opposite sex will be genuinely puzzled and surprised by an attempt to alter the current scale of values, and will see in it not merely a difference of view, but a view that is weak, or trivial, or sentimental, because it differs from his own.

But here, too, women are coming to be more independent of opinion. They are beginning to respect their own sense of values. And for this reason the subject matter of their novels begins to show certain changes. They are less interested, it would seem, in themselves; on the other hand, they are more interested in other women. In the early nineteenth century, women's novels were largely autobiographical. One of the motives that led them to write was the desire to expose their own suffering, to plead their own cause. Now that this desire is no longer so urgent, women are beginning to explore their own sex, to write of women as women have never been written of before; for of course, until very lately, women in literature were the creation of men.

Here again there are difficulties to overcome, for, if one may generalize, not only do women submit less readily to observation than men, but their lives are far less tested and examined by the ordinary processes of life. Often nothing tangible remains of a woman's day. The food that has been cooked is eaten; the children that have been nursed have gone out into the world. Where does the accent fall? What is the salient point for the novelist to seize upon? It is difficult to say. Her life has an anonymous character which is baffling and puzzling in the extreme. For the first time, this dark country is beginning to be explored in fiction; and at the same moment a woman has also to record the changes in women's minds and habits which the opening of the professions has introduced. She has to observe how their lives are ceasing to run underground; she has to discover what new colours and shadows are showing in them now that they are exposed to the outer world.

If, then, one should try to sum up the character of women's fiction at the present moment, one would say that it is courageous; it is sincere; it keeps closely to what women feel. It is not bitter. It does not insist upon its femininity. But at the same time, a woman's book is not written as a man would write it. These qualities are much commoner than they were, and they give even to second- and third-rate work the value of truth and the interest of sincerity.

But in addition to these good qualities, there are two that call for a word more of discussion. The change which has turned the English woman from a nondescript influence, fluctuating and vague, to a voter, a wage-earner, a responsible citizen, has given her both in her life and in her art a turn toward the impersonal. Her relations now are not only emotional; they are intellectual, they are political. The old system which condemned her to squint askance at things through the eyes or through the interests of husband or brother, has given place to the direct and practical interests of one who must act for herself, and not merely influence the acts of others. Hence her attention is being directed away from the personal centre which engaged it exclusively in the past to the impersonal, and her novels naturally become more critical of society, and less analytical of individual lives.

We may expect that the office of gadfly to the state, which has been so far a male prerogative, will now be discharged by women also. Their novels will deal with social evils and remedies. Their men and women will not be observed wholly in relation to each other emotionally, but as they cohere and clash in groups and classes and races. That is one change of some importance. But there is another more interesting to those who prefer the butterfly to the gadfly – that is to say, the artist to the reformer. The greater impersonality of women's lives will encourage the poetic spirit, and it is in poetry that women's fiction is still weakest. It will lead them to be less absorbed in facts and no longer content to record with astonishing acuteness the minute details which fall under their own observation. They will look beyond the personal and political relationships to the wider questions which the poet tries to solve – of our destiny and the meaning of life.

The basis of the poetic attitude is of course largely founded upon material things. It depends upon leisure, and a little money, and the chance which money and leisure give to observe impersonally and dispassionately. With money and leisure at their service, women will naturally occupy themselves more than has hitherto been possible with the craft of letters. They will make a fuller and a more subtle use of the instrument of writing. Their technique will become bolder and richer.

In the past, the virtue of women's writing often lay in its divine spontaneity, like that of the blackbird's song or the thrush's. It was untaught; it was from the heart. But it was also, and much more often, chattering and garrulous – mere talk spilt over paper and left to dry in pools and blots. In future, granted time and books and a little space in the house for herself, literature will become for women, as for men, an art to be studied. Women's gift will be trained and strengthened. The novel will cease to be the dumping-ground for the personal emotions. It will become, more than at present, a work of art like any other, and its resources and its limitations will be explored.

From this it is a short step to the practice of the sophisticated arts, hitherto so little practised by women – to the writing of essays and criticism, of history and biography. And that, too, if we are considering the novel, will be of advantage; for besides improving the quality of the novel itself, it will draw off the aliens who have been attracted to fiction by its accessibility while their hearts lay elsewhere. Thus will the novel be rid of those excrescences of history and fact which, in our time, have made it so shapeless.

So, if we may prophesy, women in time to come will write fewer novels, but better novels; and not novels only, but poetry and criticism and history. But in this, to be sure, one is looking ahead to that golden, that perhaps fabulous, age when women will have what has so long been denied them – leisure, and money, and a room to themselves.

Notes

1. 'She remained quite inert, scarcely knowing that she had a body, and without being at all able to collect her thoughts, as if someone had scattered them as the wool carder frays the wool from mattresses.' (Maupassant, *The Story of a Farm Girl*)

2. 'Like drops of water on hot iron.' (Maupassant, *The Story of a Farm Girl*)

Adeline Virginia Stephens

Biographical note

Adeline Virginia Stephen was born in London on 25th January 1882, the third of four children of Leslie Stephen, a distinguished man of letters, and Julia Jackson Duckworth, a widow. Both her parents had children from previous marriages, and she grew up in a large active family, which spent long summer holidays in St Ives. Educated at home, she had unlimited access to her father's library; she always intended to be a writer.

In 1895, her mother died unexpectedly, and soon after this Virginia suffered her first nervous breakdown; she was to be beset by periods of mental illness throughout her life. Following the death of their father in 1904, the four orphaned Stephens moved to Bloomsbury, where their home became the centre of what came to be known as the Bloomsbury Group. This circle included Clive Bell (whom Virginia's sister Vanessa married in 1907), Lytton Strachey, John Maynard Keynes and Leonard Woolf, whom Virginia was to marry in 1912, after his return from seven years' public service in Ceylon.

Virginia completed her first novel, *The Voyage Out*, in 1913, but her subsequent severe breakdown delayed its publication until 1915, by which time the Woolfs had settled at Hogarth House in Richmond. As a therapeutic hobby for Virginia, they bought a small hand press, on which they set and printed several short works by themselves and their friends. The first publication of The Hogarth Press appeared in 1917, and thereafter it gradually developed into a considerable enterprise, at first publishing works by then relatively unknown writers, such as T.S. Eliot, Katherine Mansfield and E.M. Forster, as well as the Woolfs themselves.

While living at Richmond, Virginia wrote her second, rather orthodox novel, *Night and Day* (1919), but was concurrently composing more experimental pieces such as *Kew Gardens* (1919) and *Monday or Tuesday* (1921). In 1920 the Woolfs bought

Monk's House in Rodmell, and there Virginia began her third novel, *Jacob's Room* (1922). This was followed by *Mrs Dalloway* (1925), *To the Lighthouse* (1927) and *The Waves* (1931), and these three novels established her as one of the leading writers of the Modernist movement. *Orlando*, a highly imaginative 'biography' inspired by her involvement with Vita Sackville-West, was published in 1928.

The Years appeared in 1937, and she had more or less completed her final novel, *Between the Acts*, when, unable to face another attack of mental illness, she drowned herself in the River Ouse on 28th March 1941.

HESPERUS PRESS

Hesperus Press is committed to bringing near what is far – far both in space and time. Works written by the greatest authors, and unjustly neglected or simply little known in the English-speaking world, are made accessible through new translations and a completely fresh editorial approach. Through these classic works, the reader is introduced to the greatest writers from all times and all cultures.

For more information on Hesperus Press, please visit our website: **www.hesperuspress.com**